so weird

Web Sight
Created by Tom J. Astle

Adapted by Pam Pollack and Meg Belviso

Based on the television script
by Sean Abley

DISNEP
PRESS

New York

Printed in the United States of America.
First Edition

1 3 5 7 9 10 8 6 4 2

The text for this book is set in 12-point Palatino.

Library of Congress Catalog Card Number: 00-101767
ISBN: 0-7868-4441-8

Visit www.disneybooks.com

Prologue

A note from Fiona . . .

Have you ever wished you could see the future? I have. It might be nice to know when you went to sleep at night what you were going to wake up to the next day. Maybe it would give you a chance to prepare for it. As for me, I don't even know where I'm going to wake up in the morning. I might go to sleep in Ohio and wake up in Maryland. No, I'm not regularly abducted by aliens. I just live on a bus—a tour bus.

My mom is Molly Phillips. She used to be a rock star with my dad in the Phillips-Kane band before I was born. My dad died when I was a baby and mom tried to retire, but rock and roll is in her blood. One day she sat my brother and me down in the kitchen and said she was thinking of going back to the music world. She said it would mean leaving our house in Hope Springs, Colorado, and going on the road. She told us to think about it and give her our honest opinions. It was hard leaving everything behind, but we've never looked back.

I think this is what Mom was put on earth to do—it's like her destiny or something. I wonder what my destiny is. Are we all put on earth for a reason? How do we find out what our purpose is?

For the last year my mom's been on a comeback tour and my brother Jack and I get to come along for the ride, which is pretty cool. My mom might be a rising star, but she's my mom first. We all stick together since my dad died. Sometimes my mom says she can feel my dad watching over us. That's great. Sometimes you need someone looking out for you.

If my dad ever sends me a message, I'm sure I'll recognize it because I always keep my mind open and I've seen a lot of weird stuff. We travel around the country with my mom's business managers, Ned and Irene Bell, and their son, Clu. Clu and Jack share the room next to mine on the bus. We never know what's going to happen when we get to a new town. As I said, it can get a little weird—luckily, I'm into weird.

I have my own Web site, Fi's So Weird Web page, where I collect information about UFOs, ghosts, Bigfoot, and other paranormal stuff. My brother Jack thinks it's all in my imagination. He thinks nothing happens that can't be explained in an ordinary way. But I can tell you, there's a lot that we don't know about the world and I'm not the only person who wants to find out about it. That's why I have my site—it's for people who have experienced something weird and need to know there are other people out there like them. People looking for the truth.

As long as there's been a tomorrow, people have been obsessed with trying to see it before it becomes today. Nostradamus, the famous French physician who wrote a book of prophecies in 1555, thought he could see the future, and a lot of people still believe he could. Others have tried looking at tea leaves, crystal balls, Ouija boards, even the palms of their hands.

For those with the "sight," the simplest things can be used to tell what's to come. Even a laptop could be a doorway to the future. But even if we knew for sure what was going to happen, the question is: What would we do about it? I had to answer that exact question when my mom got a gig in a small Maryland town called Dillon.

Dillon didn't seem like the kind of place you'd expect anything strange to happen. But I've learned in my paranormal investigations that the most normal-looking towns often have the weirdest things going on in them. That was sure true this time.

We hadn't pulled into Dillon yet, but someone seemed to know what was going to happen when we got there and whoever it was wanted me to know it, too.

I didn't know it yet, but things were about to get so weird . . .

Chapter One

The oversized tour bus with MP painted across the sides drove down a dark highway toward Maryland. The driver, Ned Bell, was a big burly roadie with a bushy red beard and wire-rimmed glasses. He kept his eyes fixed on the road in front of him and easily guided the bus around a turn. His wife, Irene, sat at a table in the bus's large living room looking over an account book while her friend Molly Phillips strummed her guitar and sang on the couch. A loud thump followed by the laughter of two teenaged boys came from another room. "What's going on in there?" Irene called.

"Nothing, Mom," her son, Clu, answered.

"Everything's under control," added Jack, Molly's fifteen-year-old son. Molly and Irene exchanged knowing mother smiles.

In another room next to the boys, at the back of the bus, fourteen-year-old Fi Phillips closed her laptop computer and got into bed with a cup of fennel tea. She wore a comfortable T-shirt and flannel pajama bottoms. The tea was a special brew that her mom made with loose tea leaves.

Molly said it relaxed her after a concert and gave her good dreams. Other people's moms drank ordinary tea out of tea bags they bought at the store, but Fi's mom was different. But then, she was a rock star. Rock stars are supposed to be different.

Fi opened up a copy of *The Dillon Dispatch*, a local paper from the town where her mom would be playing the next night. A woman named Susan, who was the calendar events editor, had sent an early edition so that they could see the big ad for Molly's show on page four. Fi looked at the picture of her mother in the paper. She was holding a microphone and her head was thrown back so that her blond hair fell over her shoulders. She wore a cool leopard-print shirt and a short black skirt. The ad read: MOLLY PHILLIPS PERFORMING LIVE AT THE PARAMOUNT DANCE CLUB THIS FRIDAY ONLY. It was just a little club, but Molly took every job seriously and gave it her all. That was why she was gaining fans wherever she went.

"Go, Mom," Fi said, taking a sip of tea and putting the cup down next to the silver-headed alien puppet beside her bed. "What's this?" Fi's eye fell on the horoscope page in the newspaper. Her brother Jack thought horoscopes were just made up and would never listen to anything they said, but Fi checked them anyway. "'Things are going your way,'" Fi read. "Of course they are," she said to herself. Jack was always confident, always sure his way was right. Sometimes he drove Fi a little crazy. Just once she wanted to hear him tell her she was right and he was wrong. That probably wasn't going to happen any time soon, she thought.

Fi checked her own horoscope. "'Be prepared for danger and you may avert it,'" she read. "'It's all up to you.' What does that mean?" Fi said, frowning and tucking her long brown hair behind her ears. "How can I keep us out of danger? Ned drives the bus, Irene books the shows, Mom plays the music, Jack's the big brother, and Clu—well, Clu just goes his own way. How can I be the one to save them from danger? And what danger could they need me to save them from?"

Still thinking, Fi swallowed the last of her tea. She noticed some loose leaves stuck to the bottom. She had heard that some people read tea leaves to see the future. Fi squinted into the bottom of her cup, searching it with her dark brown eyes. All she saw were three glops of wet leaves that didn't look like anything. One did look a little bit like the tour bus, long and thin, if you turned the cup the right way, and then there was a smaller blob next to it. The third blob hung above the other two like a rain cloud. "Well, that did a lot of good," said Fi. "I don't know anything more than I did before. I already knew we were on a bus without seeing it in a teacup." She heard a soft knock on her bedroom door. "Come in."

Molly Phillips opened the door. She was wearing jeans and a knit cotton sweater. She almost didn't look old enough to be Fi's mom. Some people thought Molly was Fi's big sister. But even though she looked like a big sister, she'd come into the room as a mom. "Lights out, baby," Molly said with a smile. "We'll be getting into Dillon early tomorrow and you've got school with Ned before the show." As well as being a bus driver and chief roadie for the Molly Phillips band, Ned tutored all the kids and kept them up to speed on their schoolwork. Fi was taking the same classes as her old friends back in Hope Springs, Colorado. If she ever went home again, she could go right back to school.

"Mom, did you see your ad in *The Dillon Dispatch*?" asked Fi, holding up the paper. Molly sat down on Fi's bed to have a look. When she saw the ad, her brow creased with worry.

"Maybe I should have worn the green blouse for that picture," Molly said uncertainly.

"Mom, you look great," said Fi. "The leopard print is really cool. You always look really cool." It always surprised Fi that her mom didn't seem to know how cool she was.

Molly smiled and gave Fi a hug. "Thanks kid, I needed that," she said. Then she noticed the horoscopes. "Hey, what's my future?"

Fi frowned suddenly under her brown bangs. "Mine was so weird," she said. "My horoscope says we're going to run into danger and I'm the only one who can save us."

Molly raised her eyebrows. "Sounds pretty serious," she said. "But I can't think of another person I'd rather have doing the saving. You always come through, Fi. It's part of who you are."

Fi laughed and shook her head. Her mom was probably just being nice. "If you say so. What's your horoscope say?"

Molly looked back down the page. "Mine says: 'Don't let the past get in the way of the future.' Well, I have no intention of letting that happen. What do you think?"

Fi shook her head. She didn't like the way Mom's horoscope sounded. How could the past get in the way of the future? "I wonder if the danger comes from the past."

Molly smiled at her daughter. She knew Fi was into the paranormal but sometimes she worried that she got a little too carried away. "Honey, these horoscopes aren't real. They're just a fun thing they print to sell papers. They don't really tell the future. You can't buy into it and let it upset you."

Fi shrugged. She was used to people not believing in the weird stuff that she often felt was all around them. "People have believed in prophecy for a really long time. Much longer than newspaper horoscopes have been around. I invited visitors to submit stories about seeing the future on my Web site. Some of them go back to ancient times."

Molly could sense that this was important to her daughter, so she took it seriously. "Do you really believe people can see the future?" Molly asked thoughtfully. "I mean, if something hasn't happened yet, how can you see it?"

Fi thought for a moment. "Maybe everything happens for a reason, Mom," she said. "If we knew the reason, maybe we could see what was going to happen. And we'd know why things happened." Fi's voice got very quiet. "Even bad things." Fi saw a look of sadness come over her mom's face for a moment and she knew she was thinking about her dad. It didn't seem fair that he had had to die and leave them. What could be the reason for that?

Molly put her arm around Fi and looked into her eyes. "Fi, I know things have been hard for you, losing your dad so young and going on the road far away from home following your mom's dream. But I feel like this is something I should do. I don't know if it's going to work out the way I want, but I have to try. None of us knows what's going to happen. We have to take a chance. That's life."

Fi nodded quietly. "It'll work out, Mom," she said. "You're going to be a star." Fi reached behind her and grabbed her teacup. "I read it in my tea leaves, see?" she said, smiling.

Molly laughed, happy that her daughter's mood had lightened. "Well, in that case," she said, taking the cup, "time for bed!" Molly tucked Fi under the covers and kissed her good night. Then she kissed the silver-headed alien puppet.

"Pleasant dreams, earthling," said the puppet in Fi's alien voice. Molly turned out the light and closed the door. Fi looked up at the glow-in-the-dark star stickers on her ceiling and wondered what astrologers saw when they looked up into the stars. Was the future really written in the constellations, like a blueprint for life? And if the future was already written in the stars, was there any hope that it could be changed? Fi wondered about this until the sound of the wheels on the road lulled her to sleep.

Hours later, Fi lay sleeping in her bed, her left foot poking out from underneath the covers. On the desk across the room, beside a framed photograph of Fi as a baby in her dad's arms, her laptop suddenly beeped into life. All by itself the black cover rose up slowly, revealing Fi's So Weird Web page and casting an eerie glow over the room. "Logging on," the computer's electronic voice announced.

The menu page on Fi's site had a list of links: weird stories, weird pictures, weird sounds, paranormal links, and message board. Fi's dark room was filled with the soft sounds of her modem logging itself on to the Internet: first the sound of Touch-Tone dialing, followed by the crackling and hissing of the modem making a connection. The visitor counter on Fi's page turned over from 1,243 to 1,244. Someone was there. The computer voice announced: "You have a visitor." Fi stirred slightly in her sleep as a message window popped up on the screen to tell her she was receiving a file via e-mail. When the transmission was complete, the computer turned itself off. The cover closed itself slowly and snapped shut, although there was no one there to touch it. The room was in darkness once again.

Fi's So Weird Web page had just gotten a whole lot weirder.

Chapter Two

"Clu, get out of here!" Fi yelled, waving her hand at the video camera pointed in her face.

The bus was parked on a sunny street in Dillon, Maryland, the most ordinary-looking town Fi could imagine. They had arrived early that morning. Clu Bell, Ned and Irene's sixteen-year-old son, had gotten a bright idea as soon as he woke up. He had decided to film a documentary about the Molly Phillips comeback tour. Molly, Fi, and Jack would all be featured, as would his mom and dad.

Clu had gotten the video camera out as soon as he got out of bed and had already filmed Jack sleeping, his mom making coffee, his dad stretching his legs after a long night of driving, and Molly looking for a lost shoe. To his delight, Clu had captured the climax of this minor domestic drama—the very moment when Molly found the shoe. Now the only person left to capture on film was Fi, who was not as open to the project as Clu had hoped. Clu was sure this documentary would earn him a place among other great artists who captured real life in all its glamor and gritty truth. On the glamor side, there was Mrs. P., who would be a big star any day now. On the gritty side, there was Jack leaving globs of toothpaste on the sink and not flushing the toilet. This trip had been the coolest experience of Clu's life. Not only did he get to travel with a rock band, but for the first time it was as though he had a brother and sister. Both Fi and Jack had told him how much they wished they were an only child sometimes, but Clu knew better.

"Fi, it'll be great," he insisted, brushing his long blond hair out of his blue eyes. "America wants to know what it's like to live like a rock star. How do we eat? Where do we sleep? What do we do when we get a flat tire? It's like, the total experience of a concert tour, but, like, you can watch it at home. It's totally stellar. We're gonna be famous!"

"Clu, what are you talking about?" asked Fi. Sometimes she felt that she was always two steps behind Clu, because you never knew what he was going to say next. This morning she had barely gotten dressed and was about to check her e-mail when Clu burst in dressed in a Hawaiian shirt, waving the camera. "Why would anyone want to see us living on a bus? It's totally boring."

Clu was shocked. "Boring? It's so *not* boring. It's going to be the coolest documentary ever!" Clu explained, smiling like a big golden retriever. Clu always threw himself into everything 100 percent. When Fi thought there might be something weird going on, she could always count on Clu to help her investigate any strange happenings. Even when it turned out to be nothing, Clu was never disappointed. He never laughed at her the way Jack did, he just liked the adventure. He wasn't the most focused detective, but what he lacked in logic he made up for with his enthusiasm. Anyway, Fi had learned that when you're dealing with the paranormal, logic isn't always the most important thing. You have to go with your feelings.

Right now Clu was feeling inspired by the idea of making a documentary about Fi's family. "It'll make us totally famous," he said. "It's like all those shows about real people. Like this!" Clu put the camera down and started acting out the documentary as he saw it. "It's like yesterday, when Jack ate the last piece of pizza that you wanted and you yelled at him, and then your mom was, like, 'Fi, you can't kill your brother!' That is real-life drama, Fi. That's just the kind of stuff I'm going to have in my documentary."

Fi sighed. Clu wasn't going to give up. She tried to ignore him and opened up her laptop. Clu grinned. "Okay, act natural." Clu watched Fi through the viewfinder as she booted up her computer. She went to her Web site and opened up Fi's So Weird Thought for the Day. Every day Fi liked to give anyone who visited her site something to think about. Today she wrote, *The universe is always speaking, if you're always listening. Keep watching the skies—Fi.*

Behind her, Clu moved closer for a tight shot of Fi's fingers typing on the keyboard. When he got really close to them, Fi's fingers looked like bug legs. That was cool.

The camera was almost touching Fi's shoulder.

Fi could hear the hum of the video camera in her ear. It was really annoying. "Clu, get out!" she finally yelled, turning around. "You're driving me crazy!"

Clu pulled a piece of paper out of his back pocket. "Okay, Fi. Can I just get you to sign this release form?"

Clu picked up the camera again to get a shot of

the moment when Fi signed her release form. Instead he got a shot of Fi tossing the unsigned form over his head. "Clu, leave me alone!" she said. "Can't I check my e-mail in peace?"

Fi got up and started pushing him backward out of the room. Through the viewfinder, Clu could see her angry face filling up the camera lens. From his angle, it was like watching a monster movie, with Fi roaring and waving her arms into the camera. This was just the kind of stuff Clu was hoping to get and here was Fi giving him his best material so far without even signing the release form. "Fi, wait," he protested. "It's cool! Don't worry, normally you won't look this bad. I promise! You'll have makeup in the movie!"

Fi gave Clu a final shove out the door and locked it behind him. She just knew he was filming the shut door on his side for dramatic effect, so she gave the door a little kick. "That was great, Fi!" Clu yelled back in appreciation. "You're awesome!"

Fi rolled her eyes, tossed her hair over her shoulders, and went back to her computer. Even when Clu was being a pain he was never boring. She pulled up her home page first and saw that she'd gotten some visitors to her site. Then she went into her e-mail. She'd gotten five messages. One was from her friend Candy back in Hope Springs, one from her grandmother asking if they were coming for a visit, one from a computer company trying to sell her something, one for Jack from his weird friend Myke, and one message from someone identified as Unknown.

"Unknown?" Fi said, frowning in confusion. "An e-mail message from nowheresville!" Fi clicked on that message first. She saw her own screen name, Rockerbaby, in the recipient window, but the sender window read simply Unknown, with no return e-mail address. The subject line was blank. "This is so weird," said Fi, getting more interested. How could there be no return address? Where had this e-mail come from?

The text box of the mysterious message contained only a link that read Click Me! "Okay, a Web site link," said Fi. "But to where?" Too curious to resist, Fi double-clicked on the link.

"Please wait," the computer voice requested.

"Like I have a choice," answered Fi, impatient to see where the link was leading. When the site was fully loaded, she found herself at a page entitled More Than You Could Ever Want to Know

About Molly Phillips. "Wow!" said Fi. "Mom has a fan page! That's cool!" The site was still under construction, with only one document icon on the entire page. According to the visitor counter, Fi was the very first visitor to the site. "Primitive," she said. "But cool." It was about time Mom had a fan club.

Fi double-clicked on the Document icon, which was labeled Molly Phillips at the Paramount—Review, and it expanded to a full-page scan of a newspaper article with Molly's picture in the center. The article was titled "All Washed Up." Fi began to read: *In the 1970s, Molly Phillips was an inconsequential part of the inconsequential Phillips-Kane band. Remember them?* Fi's smile began to fade. The Phillips-Kane band was absolutely not inconsequential. Without them, she wouldn't even exist.

"'Remember them?'" said Fi. "They're my parents. Whoever wrote this review sure didn't like them very much." She continued reading. *They churned out meaningless, yet strangely popular ditties (no accounting for taste) for the better part of a decade.*

Fi felt her face getting hot. "No accounting for your taste, maybe, Mr. Unknown!" Who would write such awful things about her mom and dad, and why would someone put it up on a Web site, and then send the link to Fi? It just didn't make sense. Was it somebody playing a mean trick on Fi? It was creepy to think that someone was out to get her mom's band.

She clicked back into her e-mail without reading any further and typed an angry message to the Webmaster of the More Than You Could Ever Want to Know About Molly Phillips Web page. Her fingers were shaking, she was so mad. In the subject line, she wrote YOU STINK!!

Dear Webmaster, Fi wrote. *It's people like you that give the Internet a bad name. The Phillips-Kane band was totally awesome. You don't even have the guts to use your real name. Why don't you get a life? Then maybe more people would come to your Web page! Signed, Loyal Rockerbaby, the Phillips-Kane band's #1 Fan.*

Fi hit the Send button and watched the e-mail disappear. It made her feel a little better to tell whoever this Unknown was exactly how she felt. "Jerk," she muttered. She flipped back to the Molly Phillips page and looked at the article posted there again. Her mom looked really pretty in the picture. Fi could tell it was a recent photo. For the first time she noticed the name of the newspaper the article was clipped from. "Wait a minute, it's *The Dillon Dispatch*," she said. "The same paper we ran the ad in. It's the paper of the town I'm in right now!" Fi quickly scanned the article for a date. To her surprise, the article was dated for the next day, Saturday. "That's tomorrow!" said Fi. She looked at the article again. "This is a review of Mom's show!" she realized. "A show she's not playing until tonight! How could someone write a review for a show that hasn't happened yet? In a newspaper that hasn't been printed yet?" Fi suddenly felt the whole world go weird all around her.

Not only was it a review, it was the worst review her mom had ever gotten. Only she hadn't gotten it yet. Could this be the danger that was coming that only Fi could stop?

Fi disconnected her modem, grabbed her laptop, and ran out into the common area. "Mom!" she called. "Come here, quick!"

Chapter Three

Within minutes Molly, Jack, and Fi were all gathered around Fi's laptop while Clu kneeled on the floor filming the proceedings from an artistic angle. Fi had the article up on the screen so that her mother could read it. "Okay, now pretend you don't know I'm here," Clu directed, focusing the camera on Molly's guitar case leaning against the wall.

Molly struggled to find the sleeve of her leather jacket and read the words on Fi's computer at the same time. "'I think everyone at the Paramount Club Friday night will agree,'" she read, "'Molly Phillips's performance—capped by the moment when she forgot her own unmemorable words—made us all nostalgic for the good old days, when she was writing jingles for toilet cleansers.'" Molly's sleeve drooped at her side and her face showed that she was a little hurt by the review. Jack sat beside Fi at the table. They both had the same dark brown eyes, but Jack's were full of laughter, as their father's had been, and he always knew how to make Mom smile.

"Wow," he said, running his hand through his

dark curly hair. He was angry at the words but did not want his mom to see, and tried to adopt a joking tone. "That's pretty harsh."

"Good natural reaction, Jack," said Clu, giving him a thumbs-up. "Now let's go for the emotion. Reach out to your mom and tell her that you're there for her."

"I'm here for you, Mom," Jack started to say, then he stopped himself. "Wait, what am I saying? Would you turn that thing off!" Jack balled up a napkin and threw it at Clu on the floor. Clu was his best friend, but sometimes he drove Jack crazy. Clu rolled to one side and continued filming.

He shifted the camera back to Molly, who looked sadly down at her feet for a second but then smiled, realizing the camera was on her. Clu zoomed in for a close-up of her as she gave up on her uncooperative coat and left the room to get another one. Fi watched her go, angrier than ever at the unknown jerk who had sent the review. Molly had warned her when they started touring that bad reviews were part of the job. "I make music for people to enjoy," Molly would say. "If they don't like it, there's nothing I can do about it." Still, she thought, it must be horrible to read things like that about yourself in the newspaper.

In the next room, Molly opened her closet and flipped angrily through the outfits hanging there. Why did Fi have to read that review? Molly wanted to shield Fi from the harsh realities of the music world, and reviews like this didn't help. Fi cared so much about other people that Molly knew she wouldn't be able to let this go.

Truthfully, Molly was upset by the review. She knew she shouldn't let it get to her, but that article was pretty insulting. When the Phillips-Kane band got a bad review, Rick would say, "I guess we won't be thanking him when we win the Grammy!" and blow it off. It had been a lot easier with the two of them up there, Molly thought. She pulled out a leather jacket and slipped it on her shoulders. She refused to let the kids see that this guy had gotten to her.

Back in the common room, Jack scrolled down the page on Fi's laptop. "Who wrote this?" Jack asked his sister, as he looked at the article with disgust.

"I can't tell," said Fi, looking down at the bottom of the page. "It cuts off before the byline. I guess whoever built that Web page wrote the review. He's too much of a coward to use his real name."

Molly reentered the room with her head held high and a new jacket. She wasn't going to let this review bother her anymore. "Fi," she said brightly. "You know I get bad reviews sometimes, as hard as it is to believe." She smiled at Clu, making sure he got the joke on camera. He gave her a thumbs-up and kept rolling. He thought Mrs. P. was too excellent. "What's the big deal?" Molly tossed her hair and grabbed a scarf to tie around her neck.

Fi sighed elaborately. "The big deal, Mom, is you don't play the Paramount until tonight! Hello, this is Friday. Where did this review come from?"

Clu swung the camera back to Molly, who hesitated for a second. "Um, maybe it's an old review," she suggested. "I might have bombed out here before and just blocked it out. I never dwell on my bad performances. But I remember every good show I ever gave. That's the way all the great ones work."

"Excellent, Mrs. P.!" said Clu. "Way to prioritize your memories!"

Molly smiled back and then posed in her outfit. "What do you think?" she asked, turning from kid to kid. "Cool? Not cool? Somewhere in between? Be honest."

Jack looked her up and down. "Too eighties," he pronounced.

"Right." Molly disappeared back into the bus again to change. Fi was still focused on the article. There were a lot of questions that hadn't been answered and Fi was going to ask all of them.

"You guys, this article is from *The Dillon Dispatch* and it's dated tomorrow. We're reading a review that hasn't been written yet about a concert that hasn't happened yet. How do you explain that? You can't tell me this is normal."

"Is this going where I think it's going?" asked Jack. Through his lens, Clu saw Jack's eyebrow arch with amused skepticism as he looked at his overimaginative sister who was always finding unsolved mysteries everywhere. Clu got ready for the classic brother-sister conflict he knew was coming.

"I think it might be a sign," Fi admitted. She knew Jack was going to disagree.

"Like, from the future?" Clu asked. He knew Fi was going to come up with something totally weird for an explanation. Then Jack would say she was cuckoo. This was going to be the best documentary ever. "Into the camera, please," he reminded Fi, framing her intense face to capture her response on video. Fi played her answer directly to the camera.

"Well, yeah," she said. "A pretty clear sign from the future, I think. It's got a date on it, in case you haven't noticed." Fi turned the computer toward the camera so Clu could focus on the date on the article. Then he turned the camera back to Fi and zoomed in and out on her several times to highlight the weirdness of the moment.

Suddenly Jack leaned into the frame. This was getting ridiculous, and he was going to get some fun out of it. "Oh, I get it," he said with great seriousness. "It's a laptop *and* a crystal ball." Jack held his hand over the computer screen and closed his eyes, as if in a trance, rocking back and forth. "Speak to me, oh, oracle of the microprocessor," he chanted. "Who do you like in the Super Bowl?"

Fi sighed in frustration as Jack and Clu burst out laughing. Why wasn't anyone listening to her? Couldn't anyone see what might happen if they didn't? There was a danger here, and it was up to Fi to avert it. The boys were obviously going to be of no help. They probably hadn't even read their horoscopes.

Molly came back into the room in a long

embroidered jacket, tying her scarf around her neck. "Jack," she said firmly. "Leave Fi alone!" She knew what they were fighting about without even hearing the argument. It was always the same. Jack thought Fi should live in the real world, but Fi couldn't help seeing things her own way and wanting Jack to agree with her. Molly popped open her guitar case and checked her instrument as she talked to her daughter. "Fi, honey, I think there might be a simple explanation for all this."

"What possible simple explanation could there be, Mom?" Why did Mom always have to take Jack's side?

"Well, maybe whoever's going to review my show has already decided that he doesn't like me and now he's trying to psych me out so I give a bad performance. That's how these things work. If you think you're going to fail, you'll fail."

Jack frowned and sat up straight. He started to read the review seriously this time and his face darkened with concern. Fi's weird ideas about seeing the future were one thing, but someone trying to hurt his mom was something else. Anybody who tried to do that was going to have to deal with him first.

"Yeah, Fi," Clu said from behind his camera.

"Your mom's sort of famous. People sometimes do weird things to people who are sort of famous. Even something like this."

Molly shut her guitar case with a snap and grinned at Clu. "Well, sort of thanks, Clu," she said.

Fi shrugged. "I guess you're right," she said. "But man, what a creepazoid! Who would do something like that?"

Molly turned back to Fi from the doorway of the bus. She didn't want to leave without knowing Fi was feeling better about this whole creepy incident. "Don't worry about it, baby," she said seriously. "You can't let this stuff get to you. I have a performance to give tonight, and I just have to think about that. I can only do my best. I can't worry about people who want me to fail. You've gotta just blow it off."

"Sure, Mom," Fi said uncertainly.

Molly smiled. "Bye, guys. I'll be back after sound check. Don't forget your homework. Jack, Ned says you've got an American Lit paper due." She glanced back at Clu once more and left the bus muttering, "Sort of famous!"

When the door shut behind her, Fi turned to the boys. She wanted them to know that she wasn't going to take this lying down. "I already sent my own review to the Webmaster of that site and he's not going to like it any more than we like this one. I told him to get a life and find something better to do with the Internet."

"Excellent, Fi," said Clu, turning the camera upside down so that Fi flipped over on the video. "You rock, Rockerbaby!" Fi grinned and gave a little bow to the camera.

Jack had been scrolling down the review and had just gotten to the end of it. He was definitely not pleased with what he saw. "This guy doesn't know when to quit," he said. "Listen to this. 'While writing this review I had cause to wonder if last night's violent thunderstorm wasn't a punishment for allowing Molly Phillips into our town.' He calls that a review? He's blaming my mom for the weather!" This guy was beyond weird as far as Jack was concerned, and he didn't like it.

Even Clu put down the camera when he heard Mrs. P. blamed for a thunderstorm. Nobody talked that way about Mrs. P. "Dude!" he said. "This guy's out of control! What are we going to do?"

Jack thought for a moment. He wanted to confront this guy, but Mom had told them to forget it.

Jack didn't want to cause any more trouble for her. "Mom said we should blow this guy off," he said. "This is what he wants, for us to be worried about it. Let's not play his game."

"I guess he can't make Mom have a bad show unless she buys into it," said Fi.

"Yeah," said Jack, determined to show the others that it didn't bother him. "And if he really is trying to psych Mom out he should have checked the weather report first. He's writing about violent thunderstorms tonight and it's been totally clear all day!"

As if on cue, drops of rain started to tap at the bus windows. The drops got larger until there was a steady downpour. A clap of thunder crashed outside, shaking the bus and seriously freaking out the kids inside it.

Fi looked at Clu and then at Jack. "What was that about checking the weather report?" she said.

Later that afternoon, with the rain pounding against the top of the bus, Fi clicked onto her Web site and went into the section titled Current Investigations. Here Fi described her strange experience.

I got an e-mail from nowhere and no one. They sent me a preview of the future and it doesn't look good. I don't know if it's real, because the future hasn't happened yet, but part of it's already come true.

My brother thinks somebody's just trying to scare me, but I'm not so sure. A minute ago the sun was shining, and now it's raining, just like the prediction said. If somebody can predict the weather, can they predict anything? Or will things turn out differently because we've been warned?

Why did Unknown send this prediction to me? Is he trying to freak us out and make my mom give a bad performance? Or is he trying to give us a chance to fix the future?

Chapter Four

"Dude, this looks like a movie theater," said Clu, filming the outside of the Paramount Dance Club, where the Molly Phillips band was playing that night. The rain pelted the marquee announcing their performance for one night only. A loud clap of thunder crashed as the kids ran into the club.

"This place is pretty cool," said Jack, looking around when he got inside. The Paramount Club had once been a movie theater, but the owners had gutted it and set up tables to make it into a retro-style nightclub. One of the best things about traveling with the band was that Jack got to see so many different kinds of theaters. This one reminded him of some old detective movie. He could almost imagine himself as the detective. "Here's looking at you, kid," he said to Fi. She gave him a funny look. Jack turned back to Clu, who was filming the whole thing, and winked into the camera.

"This is the perfect setup for the concert scene," Clu said, panning his video camera over the whole club. "It's like totally retro-movie-house-dance-club happening. I'm going to go scout out my shots!"

The stage where the band would play was where the movie screen had once been, with fancy swirls carved into the wood around it. The audience was just starting to arrive and take their seats at the little tables with old-fashioned lamps on them while the band set up. Ned barked orders to the crew as they worked with the equipment onstage. Fi looked for her mom, but didn't see her. She was probably getting ready backstage. Fi hoped she wasn't too nervous after that weird review. She tried to ignore it, but she had a bad feeling about tonight's performance, like fate was against them.

"Dad, look this way," called Clu. "I want to get you in action. Do roadie stuff!"

Ned turned toward his son and smiled. He always got a kick out of seeing Clu so excited about something. Ned remembered being the same way when he was Clu's age, only Ned was more into fixing machines and rewiring everything he could get his hands on. "Okay, everyone," he said, putting on an extra gruff voice for Clu's benefit. "I want all the instruments tuned up and all the connections double- and triple-checked—and don't bump into anything!" Ned gave Clu a wink from the stage.

"Awesome!" said Clu. "Dad's in control!" Clu backed up to give himself a wider angle of the stage and bumped into a small, mousy-looking man with a little beard. "Whoa!" Clu said, turning around. "I'm totally sorry!" He pointed the camera at the man and filmed him from head to toe. Something about his haircut made Clu think he didn't go to too many rock concerts. His hair had almost no color at all, as if it had all been washed out. Clu couldn't help but notice, since he had the guy in a close-up, that there wasn't a wrinkle in any of his clothes and his beard was trimmed so neatly it almost looked like it was drawn on with a pencil.

"What on earth are you doing?" asked the man suspiciously.

Clu was all too happy to tell him about the project. "Check it out, mister," he said. "I'm making a documentary on the Molly Phillips band. Well, I mean, on Molly Phillips and her family. That's us. My mom and dad are her business managers, so I've got backstage passes to, like, the entire tour. It's going to be so cool."

The man looked as if he'd just swallowed a mothball. Clu didn't know why, but he could swear he saw him flinch at the mention of backstage passes. Maybe he was just nervous about being on camera, Clu thought. "Just act natural," he said. "It's a documentary. I want it to be real life. No acting."

"So what you're saying is that you're making a home movie," the man said dryly.

Clu frowned. Didn't he just tell this guy it was a documentary? "No, it's a movie, like—"

"Young man, let me give you some advice," the man said. Clu put him in a close-up. "There's a big difference between pointing a video camera and being a filmmaker. I suggest you learn the difference."

Clu lowered the camera slowly. What was this guy's problem? Why was he telling him he couldn't do something without even knowing him? He wondered how this guy ever did anything if he was so down on everything. Maybe he never did do anything, because Clu's plans seemed to make him mad—as if he didn't want anyone to have a dream and follow it.

Across the room, Fi glanced over at Clu talking to a man in a baseball jacket. She saw a funny look cross Clu's face. He looked discouraged, and that was a look she never saw on Clu. What was that guy telling him? She started to walk over to them as the man turned away and left. She had a bad feeling about him—and her feelings were usually right about things like that. "Who was that?" she asked Clu when she got to him.

Clu shrugged and brushed his hair out of his face. "Who knows?" he said. "But he hates documentaries. He told me to work for the post office instead. There's more job security. What does that mean?"

Fi wasn't sure, but it didn't sound like a nice thing to say. "I have a bad feeling about that guy," she said. Before Clu could ask her about it, Jack appeared behind her.

"What bad feeling do you have this time?" he asked. Why couldn't Fi ever just be normal? Why was she always having weird feelings that seemed to have nothing to do with what was actually happening?

Clu gestured to the man walking away. "It's that guy," he said. "He's like, totally anti-everything. I told him about the documentary and he was, like, whatever!"

"Basically," said Fi, "he told Clu it was a stupid idea to make a documentary about the Molly Phillips band. Don't you think it's weird that we keep running into all these people who have something against the band?"

Jack looked over the stranger. He was mad that he had said something like that to Clu, but he certainly didn't look like anybody to worry about. "Fi," he said. "You can't go dragging complete strangers into your fantasies. The guy's probably just jealous that he doesn't travel with a band, and he took it out on Clu."

Meanwhile, Molly stood at a mirror backstage and fixed her hair. She didn't want to admit it to anyone, but that review had really rattled her. She couldn't stop thinking that the show tonight was doomed. Irene came up beside her and squeezed her shoulder. "Clu told me about the 'fan letter' you got today. You're not letting it worry you, are you?" she asked with a smile.

"Of course not," Molly said. Then she frowned. "Okay, I'm letting it worry me. Why would somebody want to do that?"

Irene shook her head. "Because he knew it would get to you?" she suggested.

Molly sighed. "Well, I guess it worked. But I'm not going to buy into it. I'm going to go out there and play my heart out!"

"Way to go, Mom!" said Jack, as he and Fi came backstage.

"We wanted to tell you to break a leg," said Fi. For performers, "break a leg" means "good luck." Wishing someone good luck was like wishing them bad luck. Performers are very superstitious, Fi had learned, and they have a lot of weird traditions like that. "We brought you Dad's lucky coin, too. We figured you could use extra luck tonight."

Molly looked at Fi seriously. "Fi," she said, "I told you that review was just a mean joke. It doesn't mean that's what's going to happen."

"Yeah," said Jack, taking the lucky coin out of his pocket and preparing to flip it. "I'll show you. Heads, you give the best show you've ever given. Tails—" Jack flipped the coin dramatically into the air and caught it in his palm. He looked at it and frowned. It was tails. "Um, tails, you give the second-best show you've ever given. Congratulations, Mom! You're going to have a great show!"

Molly smiled and took the coin. "Thanks, you guys. You better go out and get a seat. You don't want to miss the second-best show I've ever given!"

Fi and Jack went back out into the audience and sat with Clu, who had saved them a table down in front. Molly looked great when she came onstage. She was wearing a short black skirt, a shiny shirt, high boots, and funky striped stockings. Fi glanced over to her left and saw the strange man sitting by himself at a table. There was a pad open in front of him and a camera in his lap. Who brings a pad and a camera to a rock concert? Fi thought.

Mom started with a couple of Phillips-Kane classics and then started singing some of her own songs. Although the audience was having a great time, Fi, who had seen her mother perform a lot, could tell that she wasn't completely comfortable onstage tonight. Finally, Molly performed Fi's favorite song, "In the Darkness." Molly got into the song and really connected with the music. "'I've lived my life in one straight line, the future ahead and the past behind,'" she sang. Fi looked around the audience. Everyone was completely focused on her mom, swaying to the music. All except that strange man who was leaning back in his chair with his arms folded across his chest. Fi frowned at him. Jack nudged her with his elbow, signaling her not to make trouble. He could also tell that Mom wasn't at her best tonight, and she needed their support. He didn't want to have to worry about Fi making things worse.

Molly walked to the edge of the stage, playing her guitar, strumming hard on the strings. "'Now I've hit a wall that I never knew, and they tell me the only way out is through. Yeeeeaaaah!'" Fi heard a strange noise from Molly's guitar as one of the strings popped off and *sproinged* out from under her fingers.

"Whoops," Jack muttered. "That's not good."

Molly froze for a split second, as if she wasn't sure what had happened. The band kept playing behind her. At that moment Molly looked completely lost and Fi felt kind of sick to her stomach. It must be awful to be up there in front of all those people, making a mistake. Fi wished she could go up on the stage and help her out.

Suddenly a flash lit up behind her. Fi turned and saw the strange man lowering his camera with a mean little smile on his face. He had just taken a picture of Molly at the worst moment in the show. Why would he want a picture of that?

Molly shook her head to clear it and smiled nervously at the audience. She tried to continue with the song but, to Fi's total shock, she forgot the words. Fi found herself mouthing them in her seat, hoping her mom could see her. Looking beside her, she realized that both Clu and Jack were doing the same thing. When it came down to it, Fi knew they were all a family and more than anything they wanted Mom to succeed. In the next second Molly got the words back and continued, but she was visibly shaken through the rest of the song. "Thank you," she said when the applause ended. "Let's give it up for the band while I go change my guitar string."

"Dude," whispered Clu as Molly walked away. "That was almost a total wipeout. That was so intense when your mom forgot her words. But I knew she'd recover. Mrs. P. is a total professional."

Fi scowled. "Mom's never forgotten her words before. Ever. Did you see that creepy guy? He took a picture at that exact moment. It's almost like he made it happen."

Jack shook his head. "Fi, chill out," he said. He hated it when Fi went looking for far-out explanations to keep from dealing with every unpleasant reality. It didn't help anything. "Just because Mom forgot her words doesn't mean she's under some kind of weird mind control. She just made a mistake. Give her a break! News flash: she's not perfect, Fi."

Nevertheless, Clu picked up his camera and pointed it at the strange man, who was now scribbling on his pad of paper. Hey, if the guy turned out to be an alien with mind-control powers, Clu wanted to get it on tape.

Fi glared at Jack. "I didn't say Mom was

perfect," she said. "But have you ever heard her forget her own lyrics? I'm telling you that guy has a weird vibe, and if you weren't so stubborn you'd feel it, too."

Jack looked over at the man again. He was just an ordinary guy, kind of washed-out and wimpy, in fact. If Fi hadn't pointed him out, Jack might not have even noticed him. But now that she had, he couldn't help being a little weirded-out by him. "Now you've got me doing it!" he said. "You're a bad influence!"

Fi smiled triumphantly. It wasn't quite like saying she was right and he was wrong, but it was the closest he had ever come to it.

While Fi watched the concert, something was happening in the empty bus. Her laptop opened by itself and clicked onto Fi's So Weird Web page. The roving eye in the center rolled around Fi's dark bedroom, but no one was there. "Logging on," the computer said to no one, as the modem made its connection.

Someone was sending Fi a file. When it finished downloading, the computer logged off again. "File received," the computer announced before its top slowly closed, returning the room to normal, as if nothing weird had happened.

Chapter Five

The next morning Fi, Jack, and Clu had breakfast with Irene and Ned in a little coffee shop across the street from where their bus was parked. "Hey," said Ned, handing Jack and Fi some money from the pocket of his shirt. "Why don't you guys get some muffins to bring back to the bus?"

"Consider it done," said Jack. He and Fi went up to the counter and waited in line together. Jack fiddled with the zipper on his sweatshirt. "Did you see Mom this morning?" asked Fi.

Jack nodded. "I asked her if she was coming with us. She said to go ahead. She got back pretty late last night, I guess." Jack had hoped that Molly would come to breakfast with them. The concert last night hadn't gone that well and he was planning to do some cheering up at breakfast.

"I was awake when she came back last night," said Fi. "I couldn't sleep. She told me not to worry about the concert. She said it was bad enough she was letting it get to her, she didn't want it to get to me, too." Jack shook his head.

"Then that's what we should do," said Jack. "She doesn't need us reminding her about it. Fi, listen to me. There is nothing out of the ordinary going on." Fi and Jack stepped up to the counter and Fi's eye fell on a brightly colored sign beside the cash register. It said: THERE'S SOMETHING OUT OF THE ORDINARY GOING ON!

Fi blinked at the sign in disbelief. "Jack," she whispered, poking him. "Look!" Jack followed her eyes to the sign and gave her one of those looks that drove her crazy. As if he knew everything. Jack reached out and moved the pile of napkins that covered the bottom of the sign. He read the whole sign out loud to Fi.

"'There's something out of the ordinary going on!'" he read. "'We put bananas in the strawberry muffins! Try our new combo muffins—strawberry-banana, apple-blueberry, and cherry-chocolate chip.'"

Fi shrugged. It always seemed that Jack was right, but she knew he was wrong. Jack ordered a bag full of poppy seed muffins and one cherry-chocolate chip combo and brought them back to the table.

When they were sitting down again, Fi explained to Ned all the strange things that had been going on. Jack thought about trying to stop her, but he knew it was impossible. When his sister got an idea into her head, she always followed it through. At least Mom wasn't there to hear her.

"So anyway," Fi said, "nobody listened to me about that review from the future, but everything in it came true. It was so weird. It even mentioned the thunderstorm and Mom's broken guitar string. How could anyone have known that was going to happen?" She looked around the table. Even Jack didn't have an answer.

"Fi, it's no big deal," Irene said, pushing up the sleeves of her purple print cardigan sweater. "Guitar strings break all the time. If they're strung too tight and you strum too hard—*boing*! That's it." Irene didn't want Fi to get upset about Molly's show, and she certainly didn't want Molly thinking there was more going on than just a bad moment. Irene loved Fi's imagination, but sometimes she got carried away.

Jack nodded. He was relieved that Irene had found an ordinary explanation, since he couldn't. "Listen to Irene, Fi," he said. "She knows what she's talking about. Fi's been strumming way too hard on her brain lately," he joked to the rest of the table. "Any second now—*boing*! And it won't be pretty!" Fi picked up a packet of butter and tossed it at Jack.

"Excellent!" said Clu. "The action begins!" Clu turned on his camera. After shooting Jack and Fi, he started filming the empty plates on the table smeared with maple syrup. He thought he might cut them into the scenes he had shot of Jack brushing his teeth.

"Listen, you guys," Irene said. "Let's not remind Molly of what happened last night. Don't say anything about guitar strings or that review or any of it, okay?" Irene had watched the show from backstage and had been there when Molly came back to change her guitar string. Molly had handled the whole thing well, but Irene could tell she was upset about what happened. She didn't need to hear about it again this morning.

"Okay," everyone agreed as Molly marched angrily into the coffee shop and slapped the morning paper down on the table. She was dressed in a long print skirt with a white T-shirt under a black cardigan. She sat down and began turning the pages furiously. For a second nobody said anything. They knew they weren't supposed to talk about last night's concert, but what else was there to talk about?

"Let me guess what you're looking for," Ned said finally. Irene kicked him under the table. "Ow!" Ned said. Molly continued going through the paper.

"You know, it wasn't that bad," Clu said, continuing to ignore his mom's idea about not talking about last night's performance. "I mean, it wasn't a, you know, total disaster. Ow!" Irene had to slide halfway down her seat to reach Clu and give him his kick. Clu wasn't sure why his mom was kicking him. After all, his dad brought it up first. Sometimes his mom made no sense to Clu at all.

Molly seemed to be engrossed in the paper, but she saw what was going on. "Irene, stop kicking your family," she said. She appreciated her friend's instinct to protect her, but she wanted to get to the bottom of this.

Irene pretended she had no idea who was kicking her family. She was only trying to help. Molly suddenly began reading the paper closely and Fi guessed she had found the review just as it had appeared on the Web site before it was published.

Molly was disturbed to be reading the awful review from yesterday in today's paper, but she was also determined to be practical about it. The only person responsible for her performance last night was her. She wasn't going to start blaming the universe. "Look, you guys," she said. "I psyched myself out last night, that's all. Whoever wrote that piece wanted to freak me out, and I bought right into it. I mean, whoever wrote this—" Molly looked down at the byline in the paper and gasped. The article was written by Ty Spencer, a reviewer she had known years ago, back in New York. Back then Ty worked for a New York paper called *The Village Voice*. He looked like a mild-mannered type, but his reviews were really vicious. Molly had often wondered why he reviewed music, because he didn't seem to like anything. "I don't believe it!" she said, sliding the paper over to Ned and Irene. "Guess who wrote this thing?"

Fi leaned over the table to get a look at the review herself. The name meant nothing to her but it was definitely the same review. "Mom," she said, "that's exactly the same review that we read yesterday. Even the picture is the same, and it wasn't taken until last night! How do you explain that?"

Jack crossed his arms and glared at his sister. He did not want to hear this freaky stuff now. Mom was already upset enough. She didn't need to hear Fi's theories about magic Web sites and cursed guitar strings.

"That's Ty Spencer, all right," said Ned, looking at the byline. "I'd recognize his cutthroat style of music reviewing anywhere."

"Wait a minute," said Jack. "You all know this guy?" Jack didn't like the sound of this at all. If this guy knew his mom, maybe he really did have something against her. Maybe he was the one who had sent the review to Fi to make sure their mom gave a bad show.

Nobody answered Jack's question. The only time that happened was when something really important was going on and Jack wanted to know exactly what it was.

"I can't believe he's still in the business," said Molly, looking at the paper again. "Didn't he get kicked off *The Village Voice*?"

Ned nodded his head. "He sure did. But not until after he gave you and Rick the worst review since the night Lincoln got— Ow! Stop it!" Ned rubbed his leg where Irene had kicked him yet again. He didn't understand why it was so important not to talk about this stuff. Surely Molly remembered the horrible review Ty Spencer had written back in New York. Rick had referred to Spencer as the Red Baron because of the way he shot musicians down in flames. "The guy was amazing," Ned said.

"Even after he'd insulted the band he still expected Rick to give him backstage passes."

"Yeah," said Irene, laughing at the memory. "And Rick laughed right in his face."

Molly was so angry about Ty Spencer that she wasn't even listening. "I haven't seen this guy in twelve years!" she said, amazed at the vindictiveness the man displayed. Molly could take anything this guy dished out, but she didn't want him upsetting her kids. She could only imagine what Rick would do to this guy if he were there. "What's the statute of limitations on a grudge?" she asked. "That's it," she said, starting to get up. "I'm going to feed this guy his review for breakfast!"

Jack whistled softly. He had never seen their mom so mad. This guy had better watch out!

"You will do no such thing," Irene announced, pulling Molly back into her seat. "We've got better things to do, like go to the music store." Irene gave Molly a sweet smile. "Not to bring up a touchy subject, but we do need some new strings."

Molly took a moment to get her temper under control. She looked up at Irene and smiled. "So you're saying it would be bad publicity for me to be caught doing unauthorized brain surgery on a music critic?"

Clu leaned in suddenly with his camera at the mention of brain surgery. "Can I film it?"

Molly laughed.

"Clu!" Irene said in her mom voice.

"What if he had no brain?" Molly suggested, still considering the brain surgery idea.

Irene gave up and shook her head. "Why is it I always have to be the sane one?"

Ned finished the last of his orange juice. "Process of elimination?" he offered. He loved watching his wife trying to keep kids and rock stars under control and out of trouble. He didn't think anybody else could do it without going crazy.

"All right, Mom," Molly said, teasing her friend. "When do we go to the music store?"

Irene smiled, happy that everyone was listening to reason once again. "We'll take the crew bus," she said. "Go to the store and continue not to let any of this bother us. It's as simple as that." Irene was eager to get out of Dillon and put this whole concert behind her. As Molly's manager she tried really hard to keep everything running smoothly, but how could anyone foresee something like this happening? How could this ordinary-looking town turn out to have been the scene for such a disaster?

Jack and Fi hopped out of their chairs, eager to poke around the music store. They were stopped in their tracks by Molly's mom voice. "Don't you two have homework to do?" Jack and Fi looked at each other guiltily. No matter what was going on, Mom still remembered their schoolwork.

"Busted," Jack admitted.

"That would be an affirmative," said Fi. She looked hopefully at her brother. "Help me with my geometry?"

"Sorry," Jack said. "I have an American Lit paper due."

"Overdue," corrected Ned. Jack nodded sheepishly. To be honest, he would rather help Fi with her geometry any day. He had been trying to write his American Lit paper for days and it just wasn't happening.

Clu bounced around in front of Molly and his mom. A music store was a perfect opportunity for him to show the basic tools of rock-and-roll. He would film the guitar strings, the drums, the picks, the cash register. "Can I go?" he said. "I'm finished with my stuff and I've got to get this on tape. Two moms buying guitar strings. Whoa!"

Molly grinned happily at Clu. He was such a funny kid. She always enjoyed having him around. Even if she didn't know what he was talking about half the time.

"You see?" Irene said, gesturing to her son and his video camera. "He thinks we're goddesses." Sometimes she couldn't believe she was Clu's mom. When she had imagined having a kid, she never imagined anyone like Clu.

Molly turned to her and said in a robotic alien voice, "You've trained him well, Zorkon Six."

"Zorkon Six?" Clu repeated under his breath. Could Mrs. P. really be . . . no, that was impossible. Just the same, Clu looked at Molly and his mom seriously for a second. He was pretty sure they were kidding, but what if they weren't? They seemed like two totally cool humans, but what if they were aliens in human disguises? He'd have to think about that more later. Right now they were going to the music store.

Molly was still thinking about going to see Ty Spencer. "Maybe I could reason with him," she said, almost to herself. "Ow!"

Molly stared at Irene, who had kicked her under the table. Irene just smiled, as if she had no idea what Molly was talking about.

Chapter Six

Fi and Jack left the coffee shop and headed back across the sunny street to their bus. There were branches scattered on the ground that had been blown down in the storm the night before. Fi paused and looked up and down the street filled with people walking, shopping and leading their ordinary lives. "Come on," said Jack. "What are you looking at?"

Fi shrugged. "Regular people," she said. "Like we used to be."

Jack walked over and stood beside her. "I hate to tell you this, but you were never regular people," he said.

Fi rolled her eyes. "You know what I mean," she said. "These people live in a town. One town. Not a different town every day. They go to work and live in a house that doesn't have wheels. The kids go to school. Do you ever miss that?"

"Are you kidding?" asked Jack. "Most of these kids would do anything to go on tour with a rock band. We're living the dream, Fi, remember?"

Fi laughed. "So you never miss high school?"

Jack looked as if he was going to make another joke, but he didn't. Sure he missed high school, but he wouldn't give up the chance to see all the places he'd been. And he wouldn't want his mom to give up her dream of being a star. But maybe Fi felt differently. "Yeah, I guess I do miss it sometimes," he said. "What about you?"

Fi thought seriously. "If we had stayed in Hope Springs, I probably wouldn't have seen half the weird stuff I've run into on the road. There weren't too many aliens in Hope Springs."

"Except you," Jack said with a smirk.

Fi punched him in the arm and climbed into the bus. Jack went into his own room to work on his paper. Fi watched him go, then went into her room and took out her geometry book. She looked at all the proofs and equations, but they didn't make any more sense than they had the last time she'd looked. As much of a pain as Jack could be, she did wish he had time to help her with this.

She sat down at her desk and opened up her workbook to the place she had left off. "Find the area of a parallelogram if side A is half the length of . . ." Fi stared at the book. What did this mean? She turned the book upside down, hoping it would make more sense that way. It didn't. It would make sense to Jack, she knew. Jack was great at math. He liked the way there were rules that everything followed. Numbers were exactly what they said they were. It wasn't like the world that Fi saw, where something could look one way on the surface, but be totally weird underneath.

She gazed out the window. Take Dillon, for instance. On the surface it was a really ordinary-looking town, but since Fi had arrived, it had been one weird thing after another. Did the people who lived here know about the strange things that happened in their own town? Fi looked at the people walking on the street. They certainly looked normal enough. "And they wouldn't tell if I took a little study break, would they?" Fi laughed. She slapped the book shut and walked over to her laptop.

"Logging on," her computer announced as she went on-line. As she waited for her connection she walked into the next room. She grabbed a muffin out of the bag from the coffee shop. On her way into her room, she picked up her alien puppet. "Want some?" she asked him. The puppet nodded, so Fi gave him a bite. "Have fun," she told him, setting him back down.

Fi went to her Web site and opened up Fi's So

Weird Thought for the Day. She wrote, *The truth is everywhere, but not if you don't want to see it*. Then Fi went to the section on Current Investigations. *Things are getting weirder*, she wrote. *Just as I expected, everything in the prediction came true last night. It was like there was nothing we could do to stop it. Does that prove that people can tell the future, or is my mom right? Did she just buy into it?*

"You have mail," the computer announced.

"Okay," she said, clicking to her e-mail. "Let's see if Webmaster—aka Ty Spencer—got my message." To her disappointment, she saw her own *You stink* message to the Webmaster of the Molly Phillips site returned to her. It was marked Undeliverable. "I can't believe it," she said angrily. "Spencer has a firewall around his Web site. No fair!" Not that she expected Spencer to play fair. Not after the sneaky way he had found to sabotage Mom's show.

Fi thought about what Ned had said. Fi's dad had really put Spencer in his place. She glanced at her dad's picture by her computer. He smiled back at her with a twinkle in his eye. "You would know what to do," she said. "Now it's all up to me."

Fi stood up and paced her room slowly. "What

I should do is report this guy. I should get his server to terminate his account. I should . . . I should . . ." Fi thought of what her mom had said the night before about not letting this stuff get to her. "Maybe I should take a deep breath and not go nuts for once," she said. She took the deep breath. "Moving on," she said, going back to her desk.

Fi sat back down at the computer and scrolled through the rest of her inbox. "What's this?" she asked, looking at a new message. "I got another e-mail from Unknown with a blank subject window. What does this guy want?" Fi opened the message. It contained another link to the mysterious Web site with the instruction "Listen to this." This time Fi landed on a page for All Ears Anonymous Audio. Once again, Fi was the first visitor to this page. Above the visitor counter was a picture of an ear with cartoon lines shooting out from it. In the center of the ear it said Click Me. Fi clicked. The computer began loading an audio file for her to listen to.

The file loaded quickly, and then Fi heard an unfamiliar male voice. "Look, Miz Phillips," the voice said. "I didn't prewrite that review, but I certainly could have, given your microscopic amount of talent!" Fi frowned. What was up with this guy? It was bad enough that she had to read his nasty reviews, did she have to listen to them now?

"What's going on?" Fi asked. Then she heard her mom's voice.

"Oh yeah?" Molly said. "Well . . . I hope you're happy with yourself you . . . you big fat liar!" The file ended.

Things were getting really strange. Fi listened to the audio file again. The man in the file was talking about a review. Obviously Molly was accusing him of writing the review in advance and he was denying it. It must be Spencer's voice on the tape. But her mom's voice was recorded on the audio file from Unknown, too. How could he have recorded her unless Mom—

"Oh no!" Fi said. "Mom must have flamed that critic guy!" Suddenly Fi felt really weird. If her mom had let this guy have it, she must have done it after she left the coffee shop and that was only fifteen minutes ago. How could this guy have taped their conversation and put it up on the Web so quickly?

Then Fi remembered the review from the night before that had shown up on the Web site before it had happened. What if that's what was going on now, and her mom hadn't yet yelled at Spencer? What if whoever sent her this file was trying to warn her of what was coming? Fi had to stop it!

"Jack!" she cried. "Jack, come here! We're in big trouble!"

Jack came running into the room. "What is it?" he asked. For a second there he'd worried something really bad had happened to his sister, but she looked fine.

"I got another of those weird e-mails," Fi said. "Like the review."

Jack rolled his eyes. He knew Fi didn't like doing her geometry, but he really didn't want to talk about these weird things anymore. "Don't tell me," he said. "You got a review of a show Mom's playing next year?"

Fi ignored his joke. This was no time to argue. "Look, Jack, if we don't stop her, Mom is going to get into a fight with Ty Spencer. She's going to call him a big fat liar."

Jack burst out laughing. "Even if that was true," he said, "so what?" Jack knew it wasn't true, of course. No one could foresee the future. His sister was just so ready to believe anything. As weird as his sister was, she really cared about people, and Jack hated to see anyone take advantage of that. He had to show her that she was playing right into a trap. "Why are you so freaked out? It's not even like your magic crystal ball computer is telling you Mom's in danger."

Fi hesitated. Her mom might be in danger. That's what her horoscope had said right before all these strange messages started coming. There was a danger that only she could avert. It was all up to her. Why else would she be the one who was getting these computer files?

"Jack," she said. "I'm going to tell you something and you have to listen even if you think it's crazy."

Jack's eyebrows assumed their I'm-about-to-mock-you position. "Shoot," he said.

Fi took a deep breath. "Okay, remember that edition of *The Dillon Dispatch* that had the ad for Mom's show in it? Well, I was reading my horoscope the night before the Paramount show. My horoscope said danger was coming and I was the only one who could stop it. Mom's horoscope said she shouldn't let the past get in the way of the future." Fi stopped and looked at her brother, waiting for him to get it. "'The past get in the way of the future.'"

Jack stared at her expectantly. "Please tell me there is more to the story than that," he said. "You can't really be saying that I'm supposed to go running all over Dillon, Maryland, because of a newspaper horoscope that, by the way, doesn't even mean anything!"

Fi stood her ground. "What do you mean, it doesn't mean anything?" she said. "'Don't let the past get in the way of the future.' You don't see any connection between that and Ty Spencer showing up after all this time to ruin Mom's comeback?'"

Jack sighed and sat down in Fi's chair. "Fi," he said seriously, "let me explain how horoscopes work. They're written so that you can read anything into them that you want. With your imagination, the sky's the limit. Need I remind you that the horoscope did not say 'a bitter music critic from your past will be in the audience of your show tomorrow night and, guess what, he still hates you!'"

Fi couldn't believe that Jack wasn't going to listen to her when she knew in her heart that she was right. She couldn't explain it any better than that. "Jack," she said, "I'm not stupid. I know what I'm saying sounds weird. But just this once, can't you just do something without knowing exactly why you're doing it? Mom might be in trouble and I don't want to take any chances."

Jack looked at his sister. She was really serious about this. Although he didn't believe in horoscopes or Web sites that foretold the future, he didn't want to let his sister down when she needed him. Or his mom.

"Let's go," he said.

Chapter Seven

The music store was better than Clu could ever have imagined. Electric guitars were set up on long racks, and acoustic guitars hung from the ceiling. There were racks of sheet music, including all of Clu's favorite rock songs. He interviewed all the salespeople. They were pretty excited to have a real rock star like Molly Phillips in their store buying their guitar strings.

There were several drum sets set up on the floor. An older teenager was sitting at one of them trying it out. Clu went over to him. "Dude," he said.

"Dude," the drummer replied.

"I'm making a documentary," said Clu. "About being on tour with the Molly Phillips band. This scene is all about, you know, the strings, the picks—"

"The sticks!" the drummer finished. He and Clu stared at each other for a moment and then high-fived.

"Okay," said Clu. "You're a musician. What do you think about when you, like, play? Into the camera, please. Act natural."

The drummer closed his eyes and drummed the air a little, trying to figure out what he thought about. Finally, he opened his eyes. "It's too noisy to think," he said.

"Dude," said Clu. "That is so cool."

The drummer kid picked up his sticks and, with a nod to Clu, began to play as noisily as he could. The kid was an awesome drum player, and Clu was getting it all on tape. "Woo-hoo!" he shouted. "Free soundtrack for my movie!" Clu jumped around to the drum music, his blue jacket and wild printed shirt flapping along with his long blond hair.

Irene was not as impressed with the drum music. In the state her nerves were in, the drums sounded like a jackhammer in her ear. She almost didn't hear it when her cell phone rang. With one quick look at Molly, who was checking out the guitar strings, Irene pulled out her phone. "Hello?" she shouted over the drums.

"Hi, Irene," said Fi. "It's us."

Fi and Jack were on the street outside the coffee shop. Fi was in a phone booth while Jack watched her from outside. When they left the bus they had run across the street, hoping to find their mom still at the table, but the table was empty.

"You just missed them," the waitress said, picking up her tip.

"I guess we're too late," said Jack. "We'll have to do our homework after all."

Fi grabbed the sleeve of his sweatshirt and pulled him outside to the phone booth she had seen through the window. She slipped inside and called Irene. "Mom flamed Ty Spencer," she said. "It was total annihilation! I don't understand how this happened. I thought you weren't going to let Mom see that critic!"

Irene stuck her finger in her ear, struggling to hear Fi over the drum noise. Behind her Clu was interviewing Molly. She hoped he wasn't asking her about music critics. "I didn't let her go see him," Irene said. "She's right here."

Back in the phone booth, Fi was stunned. But Mom had to have gone to see Spencer. Fi had heard her arguing with him! "You mean . . ." she said slowly. "She hasn't left yet?"

"Yet?" Irene repeated. "What do you mean, yet?" She wasn't sure if it was the drum noise or if Fi really wasn't making any sense. Before she could ask her to explain, Fi ended the call in a big hurry.

"I gotta go," she said. "Bye." Fi slammed the phone down and noticed a wire stand full of

Dillon Dispatch newspapers on the street nearby. She opened the door of the phone booth and stepped out.

"So what happened?" asked Jack.

"Mom's still at the music store," Fi replied. To her complete surprise, Jack did not realize that this was proof that the Web site really was telling the future.

Jack smiled. "Just as I suspected," he said. "Mom hasn't gone anywhere near that guy. You're getting all weirded-out over nothing." Now that he knew everything was all right, Jack was finding this kind of amusing. It sure beat working on his American Lit paper. "Where are you going now?" he asked as Fi grabbed a *Dillon Dispatch* from the wire stand and dashed toward the bus.

"We've got to get our bikes!" she called. "Hurry up!"

Was she kidding? "Why?" he shouted after her. "What's up?" Hadn't they just proven that Mom was fine?

Fi stopped and turned around. "Mom's fine now," she said. "But she won't be for very much longer if we don't get moving! Jack, don't you get it? I couldn't stop the last prediction from coming true, but we've still got a chance to stop this one!

And I'm going to stop it whether you help me or not!" Fi turned back around and ran to get her bike.

For a second Jack just stood by the phone booth watching his sister freak out. There was no way he was going to let her go by herself. "Wait for me!" he yelled, running after her.

Back at the music store Irene clicked off her phone. She hoped Fi wasn't off following one of her crazy investigations. There was no telling where that would end up. She frowned at the teenager behind her. That drum noise was driving her crazy!

Clu had stopped filming the boy at the drum set and started concentrating on Molly. He filmed her picking out just the right guitar strings. "That's gonna be awesome, Mrs. P.," he said. "You're not going to be able to break that one. No way."

"Thanks, Clu," said Molly. "I think."

"So, Mrs. P.," Clu said, "I want to learn more about the band, like, then and now. This part is for the special flashback sequence. You know, like, where you're coming from. Where you've been. Where you're going."

Molly laughed. "What do you mean?"

"Like, what about this Spencer guy," he said.

"Dad said you knew him before in New York. It's so awesome we ran into him at just this moment. It's like the past and the future coming together. It's so synchronicity! Only I don't know about the past part, because I was, like, a baby." Clu pointed the camera at Molly expectantly.

"The guy's always been a rat," Molly began. "I remember back in New York he said we should go back to playing tunes in our parents' basement because we'd never be ready for the big time. I didn't say anything to him then, but I wanted to let him have it. Rick said it wasn't worth the effort. Oh, he makes me so mad, and he hasn't changed at all. He's still such a complete . . ."

Clu focused in closer. Mrs. P. was about to pour her heart out on camera, he could just feel it. This was what documentaries were all about. Real people. Real emotion. Real cool.

But suddenly Molly stopped talking. She pushed the camera away and marched out of the store without even saying where she was going.

"Into the camera, please!" he called, but Molly didn't turn around. Clu didn't know what else to do, so he just filmed her as she walked off down the street. When she was out of sight, Clu turned back to his mom.

Irene had just grabbed the drumsticks away from the excellent drummer dude and told him to take up the accordion instead. "So much for my soundtrack," Clu said, turning to film a banjo on the wall.

Irene came up to him, frowning. "Where's Molly?" she asked.

Clu hoped that his mom could explain Molly's sudden departure. "She bolted!" he said. "Right in the middle of our interview."

Irene looked confused. What was Clu talking about?

"I asked her to give me the history on that reviewer guy for a flashback sequence in my movie that's going to be really cool. Mrs. P. was, like, totally emotional. You could, like, feel the waves of pure adrenaline when she talked about that critic guy. She was all, 'We were in New York!' And he was all, 'You should be in your parents' basement!' Then suddenly she got all—" Clu did a big spasm with his body to imitate Molly's sudden anger. "Whatever! And she left." Clu held the camera up for his mom's reaction shot.

Irene was not happy to hear that. She knew pretty well where Molly had gone. This was just what she was trying to avoid, but the minute her back was turned, Clu said exactly the wrong thing and off Molly went! *Sproing*! just like her guitar string, she was flying through the air, right at Ty Spencer. Irene pushed the camera out of her face. "Sorry, Mr. De Mille, no close-ups," she said.

"But, Mom!" Clu began. Would no one give him an interview? This was going to be a very short documentary if people didn't start opening up.

Irene sighed at her son's disappointed face. "I'll give you an exclusive later," she promised.

She knew it was too late to stop Molly. If Molly needed to give this guy a piece of her mind, Irene decided, she would just have to do it. She supposed it wouldn't make things any worse. Meanwhile, Irene would go back to the bus and be ready to leave as soon as Molly came back. Not a moment too soon.

The boy at the drum set looked at her, hoping she might give him back the drumsticks. Irene refused.

"Bagpipes," she told him over her shoulder. She left the sticks on top of the counter on her way out.

Clu gave the boy a sympathetic shrug.

Moms.

Chapter Eight

Molly marched up to the front door of *The Dillon Dispatch* and pushed it open. "I'm looking for Ty Spencer," she announced. At first no one responded. Then a tall woman in a pantsuit walked over to her.

"May I help you?" she said pleasantly.

"I need to talk to your music critic," said Molly. "Or is he busy writing reviews for shows he hasn't seen yet?"

The woman's eyes widened. But before she had a chance to speak, Molly looked up and saw Ty Spencer in a glass office on the second floor. He looked almost the same as he had twelve years ago—mean and cowardly as far as Molly was concerned. Rick was right, this guy was trouble. Well, he was about to find out what real trouble was. "Thanks for your help," Molly said to the surprised woman. Then she headed up the stairs.

Ty noticed someone talking to Susan, the calendar-of-events editor, downstairs, but he did not immediately recognize Molly Phillips. In her flowered skirt and T-shirt she almost looked like a mom. A second later, she came storming into his office.

Outside the coffee shop, Fi looked up the address for *The Dillon Dispatch* on the front page of the paper while Jack lifted their bikes down off the bus. "We don't even know where we're going," he said, handing Fi her helmet.

"So we'll ask for directions," said Fi. "Why do you always have to know all the answers before you even start something?"

Jack clipped his helmet strap shut. "So we don't get lost—duh!"

They sped off down the street, keeping a careful eye on the traffic. The paper wasn't that far away from where their bus was parked. They leaned their bikes up outside the brick building and walked past the front window which had DILLON DISPATCH painted on it.

The Dispatch was a modern and efficient office building. Most of the people who worked there seemed to be at lunch when Jack and Fi entered. There were rows of desks with computers on them, but no one was sitting at them. The walls were lined with bookcases filled with encyclopedias and other research books. There was a big map on one wall. Another wall had a large soft-erase board with a list of stories for the upcoming edition.

"I don't see Spencer," said Jack.

A woman in a blazer appeared carrying a research book and a bag from Siesta Burger. "Can I help you?" she asked pleasantly.

"Do you work here?" asked Fi. "We're looking for someone."

"I'm Susan," the woman said. "The calendar-of-events editor. Do you have an event you want announced in the paper?"

Fi smiled politely. She remembered that it was Susan who had helped them with the ad in *The Dispatch* and sent them a copy of the paper. "No thanks," she said. "We're looking for Ty Spencer. He's the music critic. We want to talk to him."

Susan smiled like Fi had just said something funny. "Do you, now?" she said. "Well, the line to chew him out forms to the right."

Poor Ty, Susan thought, remembering the angry woman who had already demanded to see Ty that day and was at that moment yelling at him upstairs. Ty hadn't worked at the paper long, but he seemed to have a talent for provoking people. As difficult as Ty was, Susan didn't dislike him. He was his own worst enemy, she thought. He seemed to make himself as miserable as he made everyone else. Susan gestured up the staircase to a glass-walled conference room with the door closed. "He's in there," she said. "But as you can hear, he's busy."

Jack and Fi followed Susan's eyes to the conference room. As Susan went back to her desk, Fi whispered, "I told you so," to Jack.

Jack shrugged. So his mom had decided to let the guy have it. He didn't need a crystal ball to predict this one.

Molly was pacing the conference room as Ty Spencer sat back in his chair with his arms folded across his chest. Today he was wearing a plain gray suit. "You aren't fooling me, Spencer," Molly said angrily. "I know you wrote that review before you even saw me!"

"You sure did," Fi said to herself. "You little stinker." So far Fi had not heard the words that were in the audio file, but she knew her mom was just warming up.

Ty shook his head and laughed dismissively. "I can't believe we're having this conversation." As far as he was concerned, Molly Phillips was just as spoiled and full of herself as she had been twelve years ago. He had written his review honestly, he thought. It wasn't his fault that he didn't like her show. She should just face the fact that she wasn't that talented. It was a fact Ty had faced about himself long ago.

"Okay, they're fighting," Jack admitted downstairs. "But what's all that about Mom calling Spencer a big fat liar. You don't seriously think she would say that, do you? I mean, what is she, two?"

Fi shrugged. It would sound a little silly coming from someone Mom's age, but she knew what she had heard on her computer. "Shush!" she said. She couldn't listen to Mom, Spencer, and Jack at the same time. "I need to hear what they're saying."

Fi and Jack crouched down below the staircase to hear better. It was getting easier as Molly and Ty got angrier and louder. They'd given up trying to keep their argument private. Fi wouldn't be surprised if people down the street could hear them.

"What is this really about, Spencer?" Molly demanded. "You've been trying to get at my band for twelve years now. I still remember the way you panned us back then and how mad you were when Rick just laughed at you. You didn't look so all-important when you turned up thinking you were a hotshot music critic and you couldn't even get backstage passes for a—what did you call us?—inconsequential rock band."

Jack couldn't stop himself from smiling as he listened to his mom. He wished he had been there to see his dad put this guy in his place. Mom was doing a pretty good job, too. It would take more than a little rat like Spencer to make his mom doubt herself.

Spencer sighed, as if this whole thing was boring him. He certainly remembered Rick's childish display in not letting him backstage at the concert years before. It had been embarrassing because Spencer had brought his colleagues from *The Village Voice* with him and naturally assumed they could get backstage. He was not about to let Molly try to humiliate him the way Rick had tried.

Molly continued. "At least back then you actually watched the concert before you ripped it apart in your review. But prewriting a review is a low shot even for a snake like you."

Spencer sat up straighter in his chair. Now Molly was going too far. Ty was a professional newspaper man and did not prewrite reviews.

"Look, Miz Phillips," he said in a haughty tone. "I don't know what you're talking about. I didn't prewrite that review . . . but I certainly could have, given your microscopic amount of talent."

"Well, we know that's a lie," Jack said, nudging his sister. "If he didn't prewrite it, how did we preread it?"

Fi didn't answer. She was beginning to think there was something much stranger going on here. Spencer had just said the exact same words he had said on the audio file on the Web site. He couldn't have planned that. No way. It was too perfect. And if he hadn't prerecorded this fight, maybe he hadn't prewritten the review before the concert either. That would mean that the Web site really was showing her things from the future. That was so weird! But was it possible?

In another moment Fi got her answer. Molly turned to give Spencer a parting shot. "Oh yeah?" she said. "Well, I hope you're happy with yourself you . . . you big fat liar!"

Fi felt Jack jump beside her. That was just what Mom said on the audio file, word for word, and he knew it. "Now you've got to believe me," she whispered to him. "That Web site really does show the future."

Jack was about to reply, when his eyes shot up to the office. "They're coming down!" he warned Fi. "Let's go!"

As the office door opened, Jack slipped out around the desks and left through the front door. Fi stayed behind and crouched underneath an empty desk. She could hear footsteps as her mom came down the stairs, followed by Spencer. "Well, I'm glad to hear you're just as witty in real life as you are on the stage," he said sarcastically. He couldn't believe the woman had just called him a big fat liar. What was she, two? "Now if you're finished with your temper tantrum, I'd like to have my lunch without you interfering with my digestion."

For a second Fi thought Molly was going to start on him all over again, but instead she took a deep breath and didn't even turn around. "You're disgusting," she said. Then she stormed out of the newspaper office with her head held high.

Chapter Nine

Fi sat under the desk, breathing hard. She heard Spencer walk into another room, leaving her alone in the big office. Then she heard her mom's high heels walking across the wooden floor to the front door. It slammed behind her.

Fi was wondering what to do next when she heard a familiar noise above her head. It was the click of a computer modem starting up. Fi looked around her, thinking she must have accidentally touched something to turn it on. After all, modems don't just turn themselves on.

But this one seemed to do just that. Fi heard the sound of Touch-Tone dialing, and then the hiss of the modem making its connection. "This is so weird," said Fi. She poked her head out from under the desk and looked carefully around the office to make sure she wasn't seen. Climbing out, she could see Spencer at the other end of the room pouring himself some coffee and putting a covered dish of something into the microwave in the kitchenette. It looked as though he might be there awhile, so Fi turned back to the desk.

Kneeling down in front of the computer, she saw the Netscape Navigator window open to *The Dillon Dispatch* home page. A second later, the home page disappeared and was replaced by a page called Video Verité—X-treme Crashes. The site had a black background but in the center was a rectangular frame made of black and yellow stripes. "It looks like a roadblock," Fi said.

Fi started to get a little creeped out. Now Unknown was sending her e-mail messages when she wasn't even at her computer. How did he know where she was? Fi also didn't like the sound of this Web site—X-treme Crashes? What did that mean?

Inside the frame, a file was loading. Fi looked at the visitor counter at the bottom of the screen. It said: "You are visitor 1 to this Web Sight." For the first time, Fi noticed the strange spelling of Web site. "Clever," she said. "I guess it fits. This Web site really does have a special sight. But why does it keeping showing it to me?"

She glanced over at Spencer once again. He was sitting in the little kitchen area, stirring his coffee.

Ty stared into his mug. The coffee was cold. Typical.

Ty Spencer had not been having a good day. He'd gotten home late last night after that terrible concert because his car had broken down for the third time that month. It was too old, but he couldn't afford a new one right now.

It wasn't fair, he thought, as he waited for his macaroni-and-cheese to microwave. He was a good writer. Maybe not the best. But it seemed like other people got all the breaks. Take Molly Phillips, for example. She wasn't the best either, but somehow she didn't let it stop her. How could she just go out on stage and play knowing that people might not like her? What did she play for, if not for recognition that she was the best?

Behind him, Susan came into the kitchenette with her empty Siesta Burger bag. "How's it going, Ty?" she asked. "Or shouldn't I ask?"

Ty shook his head. "Everybody hates the critic," he said. "Musicians are so overemotional. They're like children."

Susan smiled sympathetically. "That reminds me," she said. "What did those kids want?"

Ty looked confused. "What kids?"

"There were two kids who came in while you were . . . in your meeting. They said they wanted to see you, but I guess they left."

"Perhaps Miss Phillips scared them away," Ty said. "She was shrieking like a dental drill."

"I guess she didn't like her review," said Susan. She sat down and looked at Ty seriously. "Ty," she said. "I know it's none of my business, but maybe if you thought of the people you review as human beings first and musicians second, they might actually listen to what you have to say. You know your stuff, but maybe you should work on your delivery."

Ty listened to what she said, but he didn't understand. How could he write honest reviews if he was always worried about hurting people's feelings? What was the point? "If they're going to be musicians," Ty said, "they have to learn to take criticism."

Susan shook her head. Ty just didn't get it. "Well, you're the critic," she said, going back to her office.

Ty watched her go. She couldn't understand, he thought. Nobody ever yelled at the events-calendar editor. Behind him, Ty heard a small bang followed by a splat. He jumped up and opened the microwave.

His lunch had exploded all over the oven. Typical.

Fi hid behind the desk again as Susan walked past her. Ty was still in the kitchen, staring into the microwave and shaking his head. What's that about? Fi said to herself. Then she turned back to the computer. "Okay, what do you have to show me?" she whispered.

The computer had loaded a video file with the instruction, "Watch me." "I can't watch it here," Fi said. "Somebody will hear me and I'll get busted." She tore a piece of paper off a pad on the desk and copied down the URL so that she could go to the site at home.

Then something weird happened. The mouse moved itself across the mouse pad so that the cursor landed on the link. Fi stared at it. For a second she thought she had accidentally gotten caught in the cord, but she wasn't. The mouse was moving all by itself. There was no way that this could be explained logically. It was as if the mouse was being moved by unseen fingers. Fi reached out and touched the mouse tentatively with her finger. She couldn't feel anything strange.

Getting a little bolder, Fi put her hand around the mouse and tried to hold it still. She gasped as the mouse pulled itself out of her hand and kept moving. Fi pulled her hand away from it. "Okay, you're in charge," she whispered nervously. The mouse clicked Fi into the video file, whether she wanted to see it or not.

The video showed a bus on a street some-where. The bus was shot from the front, so Fi couldn't see what was written on the sides, but it sure looked a lot like their bus. Then the video stopped, as if the camera had been turned off. When it came on again, Fi was looking out the window of the bus as it was driving. It was night and trees passed quickly by the window. The bus passed a road sign that read ROCKVILLE—30 MILES. "Rockville?" said Fi. "Where's that? Does that mean something?" she asked desperately. "What am I supposed to be seeing here?"

Then the video showed the road ahead. It was as if whoever was filming the video had held the camera out the window as the bus moved. The road was curved and covered with branches from the trees just as the street in Dillon had been that morning after last night's storm. The bus rounded a curve in the video and in the glare of the head-lights, Fi could make out flashing lights up ahead. She squinted at the screen, trying to see what it was. It was a car and it wasn't moving. The car was a nondescript color, maybe brown, but it was hard to tell in the darkness. It was beat up and old, and it had its hazard lights on, as if it had broken down. The bus got closer but didn't slow down. It just kept barreling down the road, moving steadily toward the other car. In one sickening moment Fi knew the two vehicles were going to collide! It was like a bad dream happening in front of her, and she could do nothing to stop the inevitable disaster. In another second there would be a crash.

"Oh no!" she said. "X-treme crashes!"

Just at the moment the bus reached the car, the video blinked off. Fi was back at the Video Verité site. She stared at the screen, her heart pounding. She couldn't believe she'd gotten another one of these awful warning messages, and this one was much worse than the others. This message foretold a serious accident. If the bus ran into that car, they could all be seriously hurt, maybe even killed. Unless Fi could do something to stop it.

But when is this going to happen? Fi thought. The bus was always traveling along the highway at night. How was Fi going to know which night the accident was going to happen so she could avert it?

Then Fi had another, darker thought. Maybe

she couldn't avert it. She hadn't been able to stop the bad review from being printed, or stop her mom from fighting with Spencer. Maybe this site just showed her what was going to happen and there was nothing she could do about it. But why show her things if there was nothing she could do?

Suddenly Fi noticed something on the Video Verité site that none of the other Web pages had had. In the corner of the screen was a small envelope icon with the words E-MAIL ME underneath.

"I sure will!" said Fi. She clicked on the icon. She glanced at the recipient window, which read, of course, Unknown. "How did I know there would be no e-mail address?" Fi muttered sarcastically. "I guess I'm getting the hang of this telling the future thing."

Fi clicked into the text box and typed CAN WE CHANGE IT?

She moved the cursor to the Send icon and hesitated. What would she do if the answer came back "no"? "I guess I'll have to take a chance," she said. "You can't always know the answer before you start something." Her investigations into the paranormal had taught her that.

Fi hit Send and watched the message disappear.

"Hey!" someone said behind her. Fi jumped and spun around, falling backward on the floor. She looked up at Ty Spencer staring down at her and scrambled to her feet. "What are you doing here, kid?" he demanded.

"I was just leaving," Fi said nervously. She slipped out from behind the desk and started toward the door. Then she stopped and turned to face Ty. Why was this guy so mean? Now that she was face-to-face with him, Fi decided to tell him exactly how she felt. The worst he could do was get mad, and he'd already done that. The best he could do was maybe listen to her. She thought she would take that chance.

"You know, I gotta tell you something," said Fi. "Molly Phillips is my mom." She saw Spencer take a step back. Obviously he didn't know that Molly had a daughter. "She's a great singer and a great songwriter and she makes people get up and dance. Maybe if you ever made somebody get up and dance you'd know how amazingly cool it is. And maybe you wouldn't be so mean all the time," Fi concluded. "Now I'm going to go."

Fi tossed her ponytail over her shoulder and zipped her multicolored sweatshirt closed. Then she walked out of the *Dillon Dispatch* office. She didn't know if she had actually gotten through to Spencer. He probably thought she was just a kid. But it felt good to tell him how she felt. She knew her mom was the greatest and suddenly it didn't matter whether Ty Spencer thought so or not.

Ty Spencer watched her go. In all his years as a music critic he had never thought about people jumping up and dancing as being relevant. Was that the secret of the Phillips-Kane band? Ty sat down at the desk and thought about it. The girl was right. He had never made anyone get up and dance. Actually, he'd never tried to make anyone happy either. He thought music was about saying something important, but maybe being happy was important, too.

Chapter Ten

Jack crouched down beside the *Dillon Dispatch* office. His bike was resting against the building next to his sister's. He didn't take his eye off the door. "Come on, Fi," he muttered. "Don't make me have to come in there and get you."

Jack had already seen his mom come storming out of the building. Luckily, she was so mad she didn't notice him peeking around the corner at her. Molly walked to the street and then stopped as if she had noticed something in one of the cars parked along the curb. Molly kicked the car tire angrily and then spun and walked off down the street.

"What was that?" Jack said to himself. "I guess I should just be glad that wasn't Ty Spencer himself. Something tells me that was his car. It looks like it's on its last legs. I guess one more kick isn't going to hurt it."

Jack turned back to the *Dispatch* office, but Fi still didn't come out the door. He didn't like the idea of her alone in there with Ty Spencer. He was sure she was smart enough to stay hidden until she got a chance to run out, but he still wished she was out there with him now. Fi wasn't afraid of anything, and if Spencer confronted her she might just tell him how she felt about him. "And then the fireworks are really going to start." Jack laughed.

Not that Spencer didn't deserve to be told off, Jack thought. Jack was proud of his mother for not letting this guy get away with being unfair, but he still wished Fi would hurry up and make her getaway.

Just then the door to the *Dispatch* office opened and Fi came walking calmly out of the building. Jack was surprised she wasn't running for her life. "Where have you been?" he asked.

Fi gave him a haughty look and tossed her ponytail. "I'm surprised you didn't run all the way back to the bus, you little chicken."

Jack straightened up in mock indignation. "I beg your pardon," he said. "I've been waiting out here in case you needed backup. Didn't you hear me say 'run'?"

"It was a good thing I didn't," said Fi. "Then I would have missed the amazing message somebody wanted me to get."

"Let me guess," said Jack. "Your psychic

friend, Webmaster of the Future, wanted to let you know that you're going to get in trouble for not doing your geometry homework."

Fi rolled her eyes. "Only you could think about geometry at a time like this." She walked over to her bike and began strapping on her helmet.

"So what did he say?" asked Jack.

"You'll see," said Fi. "When we get back to the bus I'm going to log on to a Web site you won't believe. Then you'll have to believe me."

"If you say so," said Jack, climbing on his bike. "You know how lucky you are you didn't run into that Spencer guy?"

"I did run into him," said Fi. Jack looked shocked. "I told him if he could rock like Mom maybe he wouldn't need to be so mean all the time."

Fi pedaled away down the street. For a moment Jack watched her go, shaking his head in amazement at his surprisingly cool sister. Then he pedaled off after her.

When they arrived back at the bus, Molly was standing outside with Ned, Irene, and Clu. Fi and Jack leaned their bikes up against the bus and came to stand behind Clu as he filmed Molly, who was telling them all about her own encounter with Ty Spencer.

"So I said to him, well, at least my career path's on the upswing," Molly said. "Our next two gigs are almost sold out. I guess people don't read the paper to find out what music they like!"

"No way!" said Clu, zooming in on Molly.

"Yes way!" Molly said, mugging for the camera.

"You really showed him, Mrs. P.!" Nobody could tell Molly Phillips she didn't totally rock, Clu thought. Clu panned over to Irene, who looked a little skeptical.

"And what did he say?" Irene asked. Molly hesitated. She glanced at the camera, and then back to Irene for a moment. Then she turned back to the camera and smiled sweetly.

"Okay, actually I didn't say any of that," she admitted. Then she brightened up. "But I did kick his car tire!"

Jack hid a smile, remembering his mother's karate kick to the tire.

Ned laughed. Same old Molly. "Well, you really showed his car, anyway."

Molly gave him a light punch in the shoulder that he barely felt. "Hey, don't start on me!" he said.

Fi pulled Jack into the bus. "Now, what's this

amazing message you're going to show me?"

"You'll see," said Fi. "Just wait." Fi opened her laptop and began logging on to the X-treme Crashes site as Jack watched.

Outside, Irene walked over to Molly and put a friendly arm around her shoulder. Clu circled the two of them with his camera as they walked past the bus door. "Molly," Irene said. "As your friend and probably your future legal guardian . . ." Molly laughed. "I order you to forget about this nitwit."

"He's already forgotten," Molly promised as they turned around the corner of the bus. "Even if I would like to go back in there and give him—"

"That's an order!" Irene commanded. Molly saluted.

"Forgotten."

Clu filmed his mom and Mrs. P. until they turned the corner, and then opened the bus door and climbed inside with his camera. Fi was sitting at her laptop, hunched over with concentration. Jack sat by the window, watching her. "It's a coincidence," Jack was saying as Clu climbed aboard.

"What's a coincidence?" asked Clu, focusing on Jack.

Jack sighed. "Sis thinks she heard audio clips

on her computer of that Spencer guy and mom arguing."

"I did hear them," Fi corrected him, typing on her keyboard. Why did Jack always have to act as if she were making things up? She couldn't wait to show him this Web site. Then he'd know she'd been right all along.

Jack seemed to ignore her. "Which, by the way, have somehow disappeared." Jack watched Fi typing furiously at her computer, trying to find whatever weird thing she thought she'd seen. He thought her life would be a lot easier if she just gave up searching for the impossible.

"I'm looking!" Fi snapped over her shoulder.

Clu silently filmed his favorite brother-sister show. Jack and Fi didn't know it, but they were going to be totally famous.

Jack continued telling the story of his day. The more he spoke the more ridiculous it all seemed. "So she drags me down to Spencer's office where we do a little . . ." Jack paused, not sure how to describe the day's activities. Finally he hit upon the right term, playing it up for Clu. "A little afternoon eavesdropping . . ."

Fi cut in impatiently. "The same conversation I heard on my computer I heard there—word for word." Fi wanted Clu to get the real story and Jack was telling it all wrong. He was leaving out the most important thing—the conversation Fi had heard before it happened. Luckily, Clu could see the importance of that fact.

"So it was another message from the future!" he exclaimed. He could always count on Fi to find what was weird and cool in every town.

Jack saw Fi and Clu about to get carried away, so he decided to offer a more reasonable explanation. "Or it's another tangent from the girl who doesn't like geometry."

Now it was Fi's turn to ignore Jack. She knew Clu was listening. "You're never going to believe what happened," she said to Clu. "See, after Jack took off like the little chicken he is . . ."

"Hey!" Jack snapped. He wasn't really as mad as he was pretending to be. After all, she had told off Ty Spencer, and he respected that.

Fi smiled and went on. "Then something even weirder happened. A computer in the newspaper office logged itself onto a Web site and showed me this!"

Fi clicked finally onto the Video Veritè Web site. Now Jack would see what she was talking about. She saw the familiar black screen with the title Video Verité X-treme Crashes and an icon that said Watch Me. Jack and Clu leaned over her shoulder. Jack might say he didn't believe in this stuff, but he wasn't going to miss it.

Fi clicked on the icon and the familiar black-and-yellow frame appeared. But when Fi clicked on it the video that began to play was not of a bus on a road near Rockville. It was a dog in a top hat. The dog turned toward the camera, barked, and then turned back again and again. Bark. Bark. Bark.

Fi frowned at the video. What was this? It seemed like whoever made this Web site made it only for Fi. Fi could feel her cheeks getting red as she waited for the teasing that she knew was coming.

Clu had never seen a dog in a top hat, and this was a message from the future. "We're gonna get a dog?" he exclaimed. "Stellar!"

"What?" said Fi, confused for a second. Then she understood that Clu thought this was the video she wanted to show them. "No," she said. "When the computer took me to this site in the *Dispatch* office this was a video of our bus crashing just outside of Rockville!" Fi couldn't understand why she was the only person who saw these messages. Why was nobody else allowed to see the future?

Jack pointed at the dog on the computer screen. "Uh-huh," he said. "Maybe you mistook that little dog for a . . . Greyhound?" The boys burst out laughing. Fi slumped over her computer. They would never believe her now.

But she had to try to make them anyway. This was a life-or-death situation. "I saw it!" she insisted. "It was our bus. Crashing. Don't you get it? Somebody's trying to warn us!"

Jack could see Fi getting ready to make one of her pitches for the paranormal. "Oh please!" he said. It was time for a reality check. "So this psycho Spencer writes a review before the show, then gets his girlfriend to do Mom's voice in an argument—an argument that any of us could've written in advance—and now he puts up a video of some bus crash as his parting shot to freak us out." He looked at his sister, hoping this was sinking in. It didn't look like it was. "And look at you! You're buying into the whole thing!"

Jack stood up and stuck his pinkie under his lip so he looked like a fish on a hook. "Reel me in!" he drawled. "I'm dinner!" Jack hopped around to illustrate his point of the fish dangling on the hook. Clu found this incredibly amusing and got it all on tape. Finally Jack collapsed onto the couch.

When her brother was finished, Fi said angrily, "Jack, this isn't about Spencer! The Webmaster of this site is showing me that he or she can predict the future."

Jack did not want to hear any more about computers predicting the future. It was getting stranger by the minute. "And in addition to being psychic," he said. "Your secret Webmaster can also make computers type by themselves!"

Fi stood her ground. She knew what she saw. "Well, yeah."

Jack faced his sister. He wasn't going to back down either. Clu was happy to see they had completely forgotten they were being filmed and weren't holding back. "Or, back on earth," said Jack, "that Spencer guy decided to rig his computer to go to that site if somebody—like you—touched it."

"But I didn't touch it!" Fi began.

"I'm sure when you crawled under the desk you must have touched something," Jack said confidently. "Look, I can solve this whole thing right now."

Clu looked up, surprised and a little disappointed.

"Clu," Jack ordered, "get your dad."

Clu turned toward the open door and yelled. "Hey, Dad! C'mere!"

Jack gave Clu a look. "Nice," he said. He could have done that himself.

"Dude," said Clu, explaining why he didn't run outside, "I didn't want to miss anything."

Ned appeared at the door. He wiped his brow with a handkerchief. He was in the middle of packing the cargo hold. "Yeah?"

"Mr. B.," said Jack. "What is our itinerary for the next couple of days?" He glanced at Fi to make sure she was listening.

"Tonight we head to Deer Falls," Ned said automatically. "Then we go to Tennessee for two shows."

Jack paused for effect. "And does any of that take us near Rockville?"

Ned looked quizzically at the kids. "Not unless you're looking at the map upside down. Is that all? I'm busy, guys."

"That's all I needed to know. Thank you, Mr. B.," Jack said politely. Ned went back to rearranging the gear for the trip. Jack turned back to his audience. "No Rockville. No bus crash."

Clu nodded. That solved that.

Fi wasn't so sure, but she supposed that proved that the video wasn't of the Molly Phillips bus.

But then whose bus was it?

When the boys went into their room Fi logged on to her Web site and clicked onto Current Investigations. She wrote, *Someone wants me to know that people are in real danger. A bus is going to crash into a car on a dark highway somewhere. Is it our bus? Why are they sending this message to me? Nobody believes me when I tell them about it and when I try to show them, the message is gone. It's, like, whoever the sender is, the messages are just for me and nobody else can see them. Does this person know who I am? Is he playing a game with me, like Jack thinks? Or is he looking out for me from somewhere out in cyberspace. Is he far away, or is he very close and I just can't see him?*

Will I ever find out?

Chapter Eleven

"Everybody ready?" called Ned as he shut the cargo hold of the bus. "Where's Clu?"

Irene looked across the street and saw her son with the video camera panning the whole street. "Come on, honey!" she called. "I think you've got it all!"

Fi stood away from the others, looking up at the sky. She could see ominous gray clouds in the distance, right in the direction that they were driving. Jack walked over to her with his hands in his pockets. "Come on," he said. "We're going."

Fi sighed. She didn't feel right about leaving. "Jack," she said. "Do you mean to tell me that after everything I saw you're not even a little freaked out?"

Jack shook his head. "Look, Fi, I know a lot of weird things happened here but you can't live your life worried about what might happen. You can't buy into it."

Fi looked at the sky once more. The clouds were getting darker, but there was nothing she could do. She and Jack walked back to the bus

104

and climbed aboard. As Fi got on, Molly squeezed her shoulder. "Don't worry, baby," she said. "We're putting this whole thing behind us. We're not going to let it get to us."

Fi gave her mom a smile. "Okay," she said.

"Good," said Molly. "You'll see. We're never going to hear from Ty Spencer again."

The Dillon Dispatch closed down for the day at six o'clock. Susan gathered up an armful of press releases and publicity material she'd been sent for the calendar of events. She planned to go through them after dinner. As she walked through the parking lot she noticed Ty Spencer standing at his car. The hood was open and he was leaning into the engine with his blue tweed coat flapping in the breeze.

Susan shook her head. Poor Ty. This just wasn't his day. She knew his car was always breaking down. Several times she'd given him a ride home. This looked like one of those times. "Need a ride, Ty?" she asked, walking over to him.

Ty finished fiddling with something in the engine and stood up, slamming the hood closed, making the car rattle. Susan was smiling at him kindly. It seemed that she was always coming to his rescue. Not only had she given him many rides home, but she had been there to witness Molly Phillips's chewing him out. She must think he was a total loser. "Actually," he said, "what I need is to know where Molly Phillips is playing next."

Susan hesitated. She wasn't sure this was a good idea. He'd already had Molly Phillips storming into his office after his last review. Was he hoping for an encore? "Round two?" she asked.

Ty shrugged and didn't answer. He didn't want to tell anyone what he had in mind for Molly Phillips. He didn't want to lose his nerve before he did what he had to do.

Susan pulled out a piece of paper with Molly's schedule on it and looked it over. "Molly Phillips is playing at the Deer Falls Lodge tomorrow."

Ty nodded and started to get into his car. Susan frowned. Was he going to drive all the way to Deer Falls in that unreliable car just to continue a fight? "You forget to get the last word in?" she asked Ty, hoping he would talk to her about whatever he was planning.

"Yes, I guess you could say that," Ty muttered.

Susan handed him Molly's press release through the car window. He put it on the seat beside him and put his key in the ignition. After some wheezing, the car started. Susan started to walk to her own car, but then she turned back to Ty. "Hey," she said. "Don't take the main road. Major damage from that storm last night." She pulled out a pen and a piece of scrap paper. "Here, I'll give you a good shortcut."

Ty listened eagerly. Maybe he would get to the concert before Molly Phillips even arrived.

By nightfall the Molly Phillips band was well on its way to Deer Falls. Ned guided the bus carefully over the highway, which was littered with branches downed from the storm. Clu leaned over the seat from behind, filming the road in silence. "This is so cool," said Clu. The rocking of the bus as it bounced over the litter in the road gave the video an excellent, shaking motion, as if the bus was in a meteor shower. "So, Dad, did you always know that you wanted a life on the road? Traveling the country, playing music, with your filmmaker son at your side?"

Ned considered it. "Always," he said. "But it didn't have to be a filmmaker son. Just a son who's happy doing his thing."

"Excellent!" Clu said. "Way to support my goals and dreams!"

Ned didn't tell Clu, but actually he had never expected a son like him. He was better than anything he'd ever imagined. Ned liked things to be full of surprises and that was Clu.

Jack stuck his head into the driving area. "Have you guys seen Fi?" he asked.

"I think she's in her room," Clu said. "Maybe she's cranking on her Web site! Excellent!"

"I just hope she's not in a chat room for Webmasters who send messages from the future and the girls who receive them."

Clu stared at Jack. "There's a chat room like that?"

Jack just shook his head. "Forget I mentioned it," said Jack. He walked back through the bus to the bedrooms. He passed his mom and Irene sitting on the couch in the common room. Irene had a bunch of papers spread out on the table and mom was strumming her guitar. "I like that," Irene was saying to Molly as she played. "What is it?"

"Something I'm working on," said Molly. "It's called "'Not Gonna Buy Into It.'"

Irene smiled. "As usual, you took a bad situation and got something good out of it."

As Jack passed the two moms talking, he

thought how great it was that his mom had a friend like Irene. He had Clu to pal around with, but Fi was on her own. Maybe that's why her imagination got the better of her sometimes.

Jack went up to Fi's door and knocked.

"Come in!"

Fi was sitting at her desk finishing her geometry homework. She was dressed for bed in a gray T-shirt and plaid flannel pajamas. Jack walked in and peered over her shoulder, checking her work. "Hey," he said.

"Hey."

Jack leaned casually against the wall. "So, since I haven't heard one word from you all night, I'm doing a very rare big brotherly thing and checking up on you." Jack finished his little speech and waited awkwardly. He wasn't used to having to actually show Fi how much he cared about her.

"Gosh, thanks," said Fi. She knew this wasn't something Jack normally did, and she appreciated it. Not that she would ever tell him that.

"Seriously," said Jack. Then he looked over her shoulder again at her math. "Four is wrong, by the way."

Fi looked at problem four and frowned. She

would never get this stuff. "Seriously?" she said, forgetting her math for the moment. If he wanted to hear what was bothering her, she would tell him. "All right, I'm still thinking about that Web site and the bus crash. I know we're not going anywhere near Rockville, but even if that wasn't our bus crashing, there's going to be a bus crash somewhere. What if I'm the person who's meant to stop that from happening? And here I am going in the opposite direction and there's nothing I can do about it."

Jack looked at his sister. He should have known that if she was upset it was because she was worried about somebody else. That was Fi for you. He had to make Fi see that she couldn't stop bad things from happening. "Fi," he said, "bad things happen sometimes. They don't happen because you didn't do something to stop it."

"But I saw that bus crash. If I could find the bus, I could warn them about the broken-down car on the road. It hasn't happened yet, but it's going to happen."

"Fi, everything is up for grabs until it actually happens. We make the future, we can't talk to it. We're not just following some script about how things are supposed to turn out."

Fi thought about what Jack was saying. It did make sense, but it didn't explain how she had gotten three messages about things that hadn't happened yet. Two of them had already come true. "Why is the Webmaster sending me these warnings if I'm not supposed to stop these things from happening?" she asked.

"Look," said Jack. "If there really is anything to this weirdo's site—which, as you know, I doubt—then maybe he just wants to be part of your circle of freaky friends looking for The Truth." Jack put special emphasis on "the truth." He knew that Fi hoped she could find something in her paranormal investigations that would make everything in the world make sense. She wanted to understand why bad things happened. He wanted her to see that she would never find that out.

"I do believe some people can see the future," Fi said. "I can't explain it, but I've seen it twice in the past two days. This time I have to stop it."

"I don't think you can," Jack admitted. He hated to see Fi feeling like she had to do the impossible.

"Very comforting," said Fi, joking.

"Come on, you know what I mean." Even

though they fought all the time, Jack knew that he and Fi were always there for each other if they really needed it.

"Yeah, I do," said Fi. She could tell Jack was being nice. "Thanks, Jack." It wasn't always so bad having a big brother. He surprised her sometimes.

"No prob." Jack slipped back out of the room and closed the door. Fi took one last look over her homework and started to turn off the desk light. Her eye fell on the latest edition of *The Dillon Dispatch*. She remembered grabbing it right before she and Jack had gone over there. Fi thought about what Jack said about seeing the future and how horoscopes only meant what you wanted to believe in the first place. "I know he's trying to be nice," Fi said. "But he doesn't have all the answers."

Fi flopped onto the bed and opened up the paper to the horoscope section. Fi read, "Don't close your eyes to the truth." Fi's eyes opened wider as she stared at the page. If this was a coincidence, she thought, it was the biggest coincidence ever. "I am supposed to stop that bus crash," Fi said. "I just don't know how." Fi peeked out through the blinds at the dark road. "At least we're nowhere near Rockville," she said, lying back down and turning off the light.

When Jack came out of Fi's room Molly and Irene were hard at work on the new song. "Jack, c'mere!" Irene called. "What do you think of this?"

Jack walked over and sat down. "Lay it on me," he said.

"Okay, it's a work in progress," said Molly, picking up her guitar. She sang, "'No matter what you say, I'm not running away. You're selling doubt and anxiety, but I'm not buying it for me. I'm not buying into it, I'm not buying into it.'"

Molly stopped playing and looked at Jack. "Interesting," he said. "Is Ty Spencer going to get a royalty for inspiring the song?"

Irene gave Jack a little kick. "Ow!" he said. "Okay, I get the point! Seriously, Mom, I really liked it."

Molly gave Jack a little kiss on the cheek and Jack went back to his room. "I told you everyone would love it," Irene said.

Molly smiled uncertainly. "I keep thinking about what happened back in Dillon. I can deal with that Spencer guy, but I hated to see the kids have to go through that. At least they didn't have to see me at the Dispatch Office this afternoon calling Ty Spencer a big fat liar."

Irene raised her eyebrows. "You called him that?"

Molly nodded, embarrassed. "I couldn't think of what else to say."

Irene waved her hand dismissively. "It's old news," she said cheerfully. "Molly, the kids are fine. They think you're great. They're having the time of their lives. How many other kids get to live on a tour bus and go to rock concerts starring their mom? They look up to you. You're following your dream and they admire your strength. I feel like it's really brought us all together, too."

"Thanks, Irene," Molly said sincerely. "I really needed that." She glanced out the window and watched the trees go by outside the bus.

On another road, Ty Spencer followed Susan's directions to Deer Falls. He would get there in plenty of time for Molly Phillips's next concert. Perhaps he could do what he needed to do before the show even started.

Ty heard the familiar cough that meant his engine was about to stop running. He put on the brakes and the car coasted to a stop. Ty grabbed his flashlight and got out of the car, popping the hood. He couldn't believe this was happening to him again. He was on a deserted road with no one around to give him a hand. Clouds were gathering overhead for what he could only hope would not be as big a storm as the night before. Ty fumbled impatiently with the engine. He had no intention of missing Molly's next show. He had something to say to her and he was going to say it.

Ty climbed back into his car and turned the key. After two stalls the car started up again. Once again he was on his way to Deer Falls.

Chapter Twelve

Fi lay under the covers as the bus moved down the highway. She turned over in her sleep. She was dreaming. In her dream everyone on the bus was in trouble. Fi didn't know where they were, but she was trying to get to them. She was running along a dark road, but no matter how fast she tried to run, her legs felt heavy, like she couldn't move. She saw lights up ahead, the kind you see after an accident. It started to rain and Fi began calling out, "The car! The car!" She didn't think anyone could hear her. She kept running.

Ty Spencer peered out his window at the roadblock up ahead. He hoped the road wasn't closed because of the storm. He slowed his car and rolled down the window as one of the patrolmen walked up with a flashlight.

"Is there a problem?" Ty asked wearily.

"There are some trees down up ahead and nobody can get through."

Ty glanced apprehensively at the road. "I'm on my way to Deer Falls," he said. "Do you have any idea how long it will take me to get there?"

"It should only add about twenty minutes to your trip," the patrolman said. Then he glanced at Ty's car and grinned. "Unless you have a breakdown. Are you sure you want to be out on a night like this?"

Ty glared at the patrolman and rolled up his window. "I'll be fine," he muttered. This was definitely one of the worst days he had ever had. One humiliation after another. And it all started with Molly Phillips.

As Ty followed the detour, Molly sat in the common room of the bus with her guitar on her lap as they crunched over fallen leaves and branches on the road to Deer Falls. Irene was working on the band's accounts nearby. Clu had conked out with his head in his mom's lap. Irene stroked his hair idly while she worked.

Molly smiled at him. "He can really sleep just about anywhere, can't he?"

"Tell me about it," said Irene. "When he was little I used to find him curled up in the bass drum. I guess he's just at home with the band. Wherever we are, that's home."

"So you don't think they miss having an ordinary life?" asked Molly.

"They have a happy home," said Irene. "It just happens to be on wheels."

Jack sat in the corner fiddling with the video camera. The bus lights were dimmed and he was lost in thought.

"'I've lived my life in one straight line,'" Molly sang softly, strumming the guitar. "The future ahead. The past behind.'"

His mom's words made Jack think about his conversation with Fi. Jack believed that nothing was decided until it had actually happened, but he could understand why Fi was so hung up on changing the future. Although he'd never told anyone, when he was a kid Jack used to dream about going back in time to the past.

In his dream, Jack built a time machine and traveled back to before his dad had died. He imagined them doing all sorts of stuff together. A few times he had thought, what if I could do something that would make things turn out differently? He supposed he hadn't thought about that as changing the future. It was more about changing the past.

It was fun to imagine, but Jack never fooled himself that it could really happen. That was where Fi lost touch with reality. They both missed their dad. Fi just seemed to think she could do something about it.

Jack picked up the video camera and pointed it at his mom, and Irene and Clu. This wasn't the past or the future. It was the present. That's where Jack preferred to be. The camera jiggled as the bus swerved sharply.

Up in the driver's seat, Ned guided the bus around more obstacles in the road left over from the storm. As he watched the road, he thought about the long road that he had traveled with Irene and Molly and the band. They had a lot of obstacles in their lives too, but they'd come around all of them. Rick used to say it didn't matter what road you went down, it was the journey that was important. It certainly had been a wonderful journey so far, Ned thought. It was hard to believe that just a few years ago Molly was unhappily writing advertising jingles and wearing dressed-for-success suits. It took a lot of guts for her to decide to go back on the road, but she was willing to take the risk to do what she loved. Because she was such a strong woman, he and Irene got to get back to doing what they loved, too.

Just then Ned spotted a large branch lying in

the bus's path and swerved to the left to avoid it. In the common room, Irene felt Ned jerking the wheel up front and held on to Clu to keep him from rolling off the couch onto the floor. Maybe he should slow down, she thought. They had plenty of time to get to Deer Falls.

Irene slipped out from under Clu and rested his head on a pillow. Clu woke slightly, just enough to mumble, "I'd like to thank the Academy for this Oscar," before falling asleep again. Irene stared at him for a moment.

"I guess he might as well dream big," she said, walking up front.

Irene put her hand on Ned's shoulder and scanned the road ahead. "You haven't taken me to the demolition derby in a long time," she said with a smile. "This is a pretty bumpy ride."

"You're telling me," said Ned. "In case you haven't noticed, there are pieces of tree all over the road. I don't want to blow a tire. But thanks for asking."

"This is worse than that time we had to drive through all that mud to make that outdoor concert. Remember?" asked Irene.

"Oh, the Save the Earth festival—there was so much mud somebody had to save us!" They both started laughing, thinking about it. "And then Molly wrote a song about it and it was a hit," said Ned.

"It's like Rick always said," said Irene, "'Molly can find the good in anything.' She's at it again, too. She's already writing a song about our little experience back in Dillon."

"You're kidding!" said Ned. "Let me guess, it's called, 'You broke my heart, I kicked your tire.'"

"Very funny," said Irene. "I'll remember that when it's a top ten hit."

Ned nodded in agreement. "It's a deal."

They drove for a moment in silence. "You know," said Irene. "I think Fi's inherited that quality. Every town we go to, Fi finds something exciting in it."

Ned nodded. "I'll say. She's a magnet for unexplained mysteries. I like that in a girl."

Behind them, Jack was beginning to get the hang of this video camera thing. He could see why Clu liked it so much. Jack pointed the camera at his friend and captured him waking up on the couch. "Dude," Clu said sleepily. "Did I miss something?"

"Nothing much," said Jack, from behind the camera. "I've decided to do my own documentary.

The subject will be 'The Making of . . . Clu's Documentary.'"

Clu took a moment to process this and then he jumped up. "Stellar! What do I do?"

"You sit there," said Jack, motioning to a chair. "And let me interview you." Clu flopped into the chair. "So tell me, Mr. Bell, what inspired you to make your Oscar-winning documentary?"

Clu happily answered. "Okay, see, I was brushing my teeth and I thought, whoa, I'm brushing my teeth in a bus! The world should know about this. Then the whole thing, like, took off! It was like brushing your teeth, and Molly Phillips and rock-and-roll, and I knew it would be the coolest documentary ever! And we all get to be in it!" Clu grinned widely at the camera.

Jack nodded. "Fascinating." Only Clu could look at a toothbrush and see a whole documentary. "And then what happened?" he asked.

"So then I started seeing all the cool stuff that goes on around here and I wanted to get it all on video. I got Mrs. P. peeling a banana, and my dad drinking coffee. Oh, and then one night I was filming you sleep—"

"What?" said Jack, looking at Clu from behind the camera.

"Dude, I wanted to get you doing all that weird stuff you do in your sleep. You know, like mumbling and talking and stuff."

"I do not mumble and talk in my sleep," Jack said firmly.

"You want to see the tape?" Clu said happily. "I've got you saying all this stuff about cowboys and high noon. It was excellent!"

Jack felt his face getting red. "No way I would say that," he said, a little less firmly. Actually, just the other night he had dreamed he was Wyatt Earp and he had run a low-down varmint out of town for disorderly behavior and—"Clu, if you ever let anybody see that tape . . ." he began.

"Dude," Clu reminded him. "You signed a release form!" The two boys looked at each other for a moment and then Jack sprang up, as if he was going to grab Clu. Clu jumped up out of his reach, pretending to be scared.

Jack gave Clu a look as if to say, "I haven't forgotten about this," and then turned back to the video camera. He himself wasn't as interested in filming the goings-on inside the bus as Clu was. He pointed the camera out the window and filmed the broken trees on the wet road. He saw flashing lights up ahead. A roadblock was set up around some fallen power lines. The bus slowed to a stop.

"What's the problem?" Ned asked a state trooper holding a flashlight.

"The road's closed up ahead," the man said. "Detour off that way." He pointed to a turnoff and waved his flashlight.

Ned eyed it cautiously. "We're on our way to Deer Falls. Do you think I'll have any trouble in this rig?"

The trooper checked out the size of the bus. "That's a pretty big vehicle," he admitted. "But the detour's clear. Hey, what's the MP stand for?"

"Molly Phillips," Irene said, poking her head out. "We're the Molly Phillips band."

The state trooper broke into a smile. "No kidding?" he said. "I saw the Phillips-Kane band play once in Milwaukee. You rocked the house!"

Irene grinned. "Lucky we ran into you."

"You bet," the man said. "You're only the second vehicle to come through here all night. The first one was a guy in a car that looked like it might not make it much farther. He was on his way to Deer Falls, too. You might have to give him a ride up ahead."

"No problem," said Ned. "As long as he doesn't mind carrying some equipment for us."

The trooper laughed. He couldn't wait to get home and tell his wife he'd seen Molly Phillips's tour bus.

Ned steered the bus onto the turnoff. "Hey, do you know why the kids would be interested in Rockville?" he asked.

Irene frowned. "I don't know. Why?"

"Well, this afternoon Jack asked me if we would be going anywhere near Rockville."

"That's strange," said Irene. "We're not going there, are we?"

"We are now," said Ned. "This detour will take us right by it."

Chapter Thirteen

Ty Spencer was stuck again. His car had died soon after he'd been stopped at the roadblock. He turned on his hazard lights and tried the engine as usual, but this time it looked like it wasn't going to get started again. Ty kicked his car tire in frustration.

What was he going to do now? He was beginning to seriously regret going after Molly Phillips and her band. "No, I have to do it," he said out loud. "I just have to." Ty walked around to the trunk of his car, looking for the flares he usually carried. Of course he'd forgotten them.

He had no idea how he was going to get out of this mess. He could only hope that someone would come along and give him a ride to a telephone.

Back in the Molly Phillips tour bus, Jack was hanging out the window filming with the video camera. Clu had his head stuck out the window in front so Jack could film him too.

"Woo-hoo!" shouted Clu, his blond hair whipping around his head in the light rain that was starting to fall. "The inside! The outside! I'm in both worlds at once!"

"You're in a different world, all right," called Jack. "Ground control to Major Clu!"

"Hold it!" Clu said. "I've got a brilliant idea!"

Clu ducked his head back into the bus and ran back toward the other end of the bus. He reached up to a shelf and pulled down a stuffed grasshopper that Molly had won by knocking over milk bottles at a county fair in Minnesota. Fi liked it because she said it looked like an alien with its little head, long, skinny legs, and antennae. "You're going to be a star!" Clu told the grasshopper, running back to the window. "Jack, get this! The bus is being attacked by giant grasshoppers! Who will save us?"

Jack zoomed in on the face of the stuffed grasshopper so that it looked huge. He spoke in a deep, threatening voice that was supposed to belong to the grasshopper. "So, we meet again, Mr. Phillips," the grasshopper said. "I have come to exact revenge for all the bugs that have lost their lives on the windshield of sudden death!"

Clu stuck his own face into the camera lens. "The horror! The horror!" Suddenly Clu pretended to be attacked by the vicious grasshopper he was holding. With the stuffed bug stuck to his face, he fell to the floor and writhed while Jack filmed the struggle from above. The grasshopper won, and Clu collapsed onto the floor.

"And so ends the battle between man and insect," Jack said solemnly, narrating the scene. "Man goes from being master of his own destiny, to splat on a tour bus floor."

Jack heard applause from the other side of the room. Molly and Irene were watching the scene with amusement. "Very nice, Mr. Hitchcock," Molly said. "The road's bumpy up ahead. Maybe you should take your seats."

"That means you, too, Clu," Irene said. Clu opened one eye.

"You heard her," he said to the grasshopper, getting up off the floor. Jack went to the window again and began filming the road outside. Now that he had gotten the hang of it, this video camera was pretty cool. He was starting to think Clu had a good idea, when he decided to make a documentary of the band on tour.

"Hey, Mrs. P.," said Clu. "How about writing something for, like, a theme song for the documentary?"

Molly picked up her guitar and sang, "'We

were bouncing down the highway, I heard something call my name. It was green and had antennae, the night the grasshoppers came! Yeeeeaaah!'"

Clu was overcome with Molly's song. Even Jack turned from the window and applauded.

Fi was sleeping soundly in her room. The lights along the highway flashed through the blinds, making patterns on the walls. On her desk by the window, her laptop began to open slowly by itself as if unseen hands were lifting up the cover. The computer clicked on and soon the familiar sight of Fi's So Weird Web page appeared on the screen. The roving eye in the "O" circled around, as if it were checking out Fi's room.

There was a beep and a hiss as the computer logged itself on to the Internet. It was louder than usual, as if someone wanted Fi to hear it. What was the computer connecting to? Was it really the Internet, or somewhere far beyond? Fi shifted in her sleep, almost hearing the strange noise. "Logging on," a mechanical voice announced. Fi turned over.

Almost as soon as the computer had logged on, the voice said, "You have mail!" A box appeared on the computer. "Receiving file," the voice said. The box on the screen showed a file of some kind being sent into Fi's computer. The box contained an empty bar that filled as the file was received. Underneath, a counter indicated how much of the file had been received: 10%, 25%, 50%. "Message received," the computer said as the counter reached 100%.

Fi stirred and opened her eyes. She saw her computer sitting open on her desk. "I'm sure I closed it," she mumbled. She squinted at the screen. Instead of her Web site, a window opened in the middle of the screen and a video began to play. "That's it!" Fi exclaimed, jumping out of bed and hurrying to the computer.

It was exactly the same video she had seen on the computer in the *Dillon Dispatch* office. Once again, she saw a bus on a road somewhere. Fi looked closely at the front of the bus. Was that Ned in the driver's seat, or was it her imagination? Then the video cut to a shot of night and trees passing quickly by the window. "Just like they are now," Fi said. "This is so weird."

The bus in the video passed the road sign Fi remembered that read ROCKVILLE—30 MILES. Instinctively, Fi glanced out her own window and gasped. Just at that moment her own bus passed the same sign indicating that Rockville was thirty miles away. "Rockville!" said Fi. "But Ned said we weren't going anywhere near Rockville!"

But the bus was heading for Rockville fast and unless Fi could stop it, she knew they were going to crash.

Chapter Fourteen

Ty Spencer wiped his brow. He'd been trying to push his car off the road so other drivers wouldn't be in danger of running into it. "I ought to just leave you here," he said to the car. "You couldn't take me a few more miles?"

There was nothing else he could do until someone else came by, so he just kept trying to push the car. It was beginning to rain again and the raindrops fell into the collar of his shirt and ran down his neck. His stomach rumbled. He hadn't had any dinner and his lunch had exploded all over the microwave at work. He reached into his pocket, pulled out half a candy bar, and munched on it miserably.

Molly had just found the perfect chord to end her new song. She leaned over her music pad and made a note of it. Then she played the last few lines for Irene. "'No matter what you say, I'm not running away. You're selling doubt and anxiety, but I'm not buying it for me. I'm not buying into it, I'm not buying into it.'"

Irene applauded and offered Molly a piece of gum for a song well written.

"You know, this would kill Spencer," Molly said. "This is one of the best songs I've ever written. If it becomes a hit, he'll have to know he was the inspiration."

"So you see, it was good luck that we ran into him," said Jack.

Irene laughed. "Imagine him driving along in his car and hearing it come on the radio," she said. "Ty Spencer, this one's for you!"

Molly and Irene both laughed. "Well, it serves him right," said Molly. "That review he wrote was way out of line, no matter when he wrote it."

"I feel kind of sorry for the guy," Irene said. Jack raised his eyebrows. "I do," she said. "Imagine not being able to appreciate a good show. He spends all his time looking for something not to like in everything he sees or hears."

"And then he gets mad when other people don't listen to him," said Jack. "And the madder he gets, the less people listen."

Molly looked thoughtful. "I guess things aren't going very well for him," she said. "When I kicked his tire his car looked like it was on its last legs," she said. "And here we are sitting around a table in our nice warm bus."

"Don't worry, Molly," Irene said with a smile.

"I'm sure Spencer's warm and comfortable wherever he is."

Ty sneezed and walked around the side of his car, stepping in a puddle. By now he was so wet he didn't care. He looked around the curve in the road where his car had stalled, hoping to see someone coming to his rescue, but the highway was empty. "Who else but me would be crazy enough to be out on a night like this?" Ty said. Still, he had good reason to be out in the rain and he knew it. Soon Molly Phillips would know it, too. That is, if he ever got to Deer Falls.

Ned squinted through the falling rain. He didn't want to miss any of the branches on the road. This was definitely not a good night to get a flat tire. In his mind he was going over all the things he had to do to prepare for Molly's show in Deer Falls. He had to remember to tell Irene to order a bunch of supplies.

Irene was planning how they would market Molly's new song. She hoped it would be ready for Molly to sing it by the time they got to Tennessee. She was sure the band would be eager to learn it. A new song would be just the thing to make everyone forget the Dillon Disaster, as the band had begun to jokingly refer to it. "Molly, I think on that last chorus . . ." she began.

Suddenly Fi's door slammed open and she stumbled out. Everyone was sitting around the common room as if it was any other night. Had she dreamed getting that strange message on her computer? Looking to the left, she saw Jack leaning out the window. "Jack?" she said uncertainly. Maybe he could tell her how they had gotten on the road to Rockville. "When did we—" Fi stopped short. Jack was holding the video camera out the window, and filming the road ahead—the road ahead! "What are you doing?" Fi whispered.

Jack pulled his head in. His hair was stuck to his head from the rain outside. When he looked at his sister, he could see something was wrong. Her face was pale and she looked dazed, like she was walking in her sleep or something. "What's wrong?" he asked with concern.

Fi just stared at the camera. "What are you doing?" she repeated.

Jack shrugged. "Hey, Clu gets to play around with the camera all the time . . ." What was up with Fi? Why was she so weirded-out by seeing Jack with the camera?

Fi felt the familiar lean of the bus about to make a wide turn to the left. When you live on a bus, you learn to make quick adjustments. Almost without thinking about it, everyone braced themselves. Jack automatically put his hand on the can of pencils to keep it from falling off the counter. Irene held her papers in place. Molly shifted in her seat with her guitar.

Suddenly, everything made terrible sense to Fi. The bus was making a left turn, just like the one in the video. They had just passed the sign to Rockville. That meant that just around the corner where Ned couldn't see it was . . . Could they really be about to hit another car in the road? Fi thought of her horoscopes for the past two days. "Be prepared for danger and you may avert it. It's all up to you." "Don't close your eyes to the truth." It was a warning, and now it was all up to Fi.

"Mom," Fi whimpered. "The car, Mom, the car."

Molly looked at Fi and saw something was terribly wrong. "Fi, what is it?" she said, hurrying over to her. "Baby, what's wrong?" Molly started to reach out to her but Fi turned away.

More than anything else, Fi wanted to tell her mother what was wrong, but she suddenly realized that there was no time. She had to get to the front of the bus and stop Ned. She started running toward Ned at the wheel. It was strange, Fi thought, because even though she was running she felt like she was moving in slow motion. It was almost like a dream where you're desperately trying to run but you can't get anywhere. Ned seemed like he was miles away from her, even though she was almost upon him.

Jack pulled the camera down from his face. "Fi, what is it?" he asked. Why didn't she tell him what was going on? She looked really upset. This was clearly not Fi letting her imagination run away with her. But Jack couldn't see anything wrong. The bus was moving along like always and everyone was fine. What was making Fi act this way?

"The car!" she screamed again. "There's going to be a car! Look out for the car!"

Now Irene was concerned about Fi. She'd never seen her like this before. She looked scared to death. "Fi, what's wrong?" she began, but Fi didn't seem to hear her. Irene thought maybe Fi was sleepwalking or had had a bad dream.

"Watch out for the car!"

Ned whipped his head around toward Fi's

voice. "What?" he said. As he turned around Fi ran up and grabbed the wheel. Ned couldn't believe it—she had never done anything like this before. He looked at Fi, who had a wild look in her eyes. There was no time to ask her what was wrong, because the bus was going out of control. Ned did not see the beat-up car stalled in the road directly in the path of the speeding bus.

"Fi, what are you doing?" Molly said, running up behind her. Fi knew better than to grab the wheel while Ned was driving.

Fi didn't answer. She just yanked the wheel sharply to the right. She knew what she was doing was dangerous, but it was the only thing that would save them. She couldn't believe how hard it was to turn the wheel. The extra-large bus was so heavy she had to pull with all her might to get it to turn in time.

"Fiona!" Ned yelled, afraid that they were going to crash.

Molly fell back as the bus swerved. Irene grabbed hold of Clu and they both flew off the couch onto the floor. Jack fell backward with the video camera. The lens cap swung wildly. The grasshopper slid across the table where Clu had placed it and bounced onto the floor.

Ned stared in horror in front of him—there was a car in the road, directly in his path! He grabbed the wheel along with Fi and together they turned it to the right.

Ty heard the rumble of the bus coming down the road. Finally, he thought, someone to help me.

But when Ty turned and saw the huge bus barreling down at him, he knew this really was the worst day of his life—and maybe the last. The bus was coming so fast there was no time for him to run. His feet seemed to be frozen to the highway. As the bus bore down on him he realized that he would never complete his mission of that night. He would never complete anything again. This was where it would end. How did he get from *The Village Voice* to this lonely highway and certain death?

Staring up at the bus, Ty was vaguely aware of two people sitting in the driver's seat. Just as it was about to make contact with Ty's car, the front swerved, barely missing his bumper. Unbelievably, the bus missed his car, just scraping by along the guardrail with a metallic screech. He shut his eyes until the noise stopped and he knew that he was safe.

Ned pressed his large foot on the brake,

pushing the pedal into the floor. The big wheels of the bus locked and skidded across the road. Smoke poured from the tires as the rubber burned on the asphalt with a squeal. Gravel sprayed across the road.

The bus cleared the stalled car, and was now sliding toward the trees on the other side of the road. Ned struggled with the wheel, forcing it away from a head-on collision. His burly arms strained against the wheel. Fi held tight and tried to help him, gritting her teeth. Tree branches slapped against the bus windows.

With a final loud scraping sound the bus came to a stop on the roadside opposite Ty's car. For a moment, Ned and Fi silently stared out the window.

Fi couldn't believe it was over. Her hands were still gripping the steering wheel and her arms were shaking. Actually, she was shaking all over.

Molly pulled herself to her feet from where she had fallen. Irene, still holding Clu on the floor of the bus, checked him for bumps and bruises. "Whoa," he said. "Did we hit an iceberg?"

Jack tried to pull himself up in one quick move, but his legs were rubbery and he fell back down onto the floor. "I think I'll stay down here," he said to himself. "Until my legs are ready to work again."

Molly hurried toward the driver's seat. "Are you okay? What happened?" she asked Fi.

Fi and Ned turned to each other, both still holding on to the wheel for dear life. Ned looked at Fi in disbelief.

"How did you know?" he said.

Chapter Fifteen

As soon as it was clear nobody was hurt, Molly and Ned ran out of the bus to see if the other driver was okay. They were soon followed by Irene and the boys. "I'm okay, Mom," Jack said as Molly threw her arms around him. She held him tightly. "I'm okay." Now that they were safe, Molly was starting to realize how close to real disaster they had come and she wanted to hold everyone close.

Ned gave Clu a hug. "Don't worry, Dad," he said brightly. "Excellent team driving!" Somehow Ned knew that Clu would take this whole thing in stride. Ned himself was still shaking. He gave Clu another hug for good measure.

Molly ran toward the other car, which was so beat-up it almost looked as if it had been hit by a bus already. The driver walked shakily toward her through the smoke pouring out of the engine. It was a man in a wrinkled wet suit. His hair was plastered to his head. "The poor guy," Molly said to herself. "He looks like a drowned rat."

Molly stopped short. She couldn't believe who she was seeing stumbling toward her on the road.

It was Ty Spencer, the same guy she had been chewing out that afternoon. What was he doing out here on the road to Deer Falls? "Spencer?" she said. "What are you doing here?"

"Are you all right?" Ned asked. He had just recognized the music critic himself. Ty nodded mutely. For the first time, he was completely at a loss for words. He had just been thinking about Molly Phillips, and then he was almost run over, and now here was Molly Phillips again asking him if he was okay? This whole night was beginning to seem like a crazy dream.

Fi stepped out of the bus. She still felt a little bit lost in a dream herself. She was so cold, she felt that she would never get warm. She had wrapped a heavy blanket from the bus around her shoulders. She looked frantically around the road, seeing Irene, Ned, Clu, and Jack. Then she saw her mother talking to a man in a rumpled dark suit. It must be the driver of the stalled car, Fi thought. Wait a minute! It was Ty Spencer! This was so weird. How could he be the person Fi was supposed to save? Who planned that?

"Jack, do you see who that is?" she asked her brother. "It's that critic guy!"

Jack stiffened. He didn't like his mom talking

143

to that guy. If Spencer insulted her again he'd have Jack to answer to.

"Dudes, check it out," said Clu, pointing to Spencer. "It's the guy from the concert—the guy who didn't like my movie!"

Fi and Jack nodded. "That's the guy who flamed Mom in his column," said Jack.

"Do you think Mom needs our help?" said Fi.

Jack shook his head. "Mom can take care of herself," he said. "Let her work it out with this guy. I think that's the way Mom wants it."

Beside them Ned and Irene were having a similar discussion. "I can't believe I almost ran into him," said Ned in a shaky voice.

Irene looked worried. "He might have more than that to worry about now that Molly's caught up with him," Irene said. "I wonder what they're talking about."

"What are you doing here, Spencer?" Molly asked again.

Ty took a deep breath. "I was trying to catch up with you," he said. "I wanted to come to your show in Deer Falls."

Molly frowned. Was Spencer actually following her to the next town just to give her another bad review? She got ready to let him have it.

"It's not like that," Ty said quickly. He supposed Molly had good reason to believe the worst of him. "I wanted to apologize."

For a second Molly was so stunned she didn't know what to say. She'd known this guy for years and she'd never heard of him apologizing to anybody, and it wasn't as though Molly was the first person he'd run up against. "You wanted to apologize to me?" she said finally.

"Yes," said Ty. "Someone pointed out to me today that your music makes people get up and dance. I guess that's what music is supposed to do. I don't know when it happened, but somewhere along the way, I lost sight of why I loved music in the first place. I stopped being a music critic and started looking for reasons to put things down. After a while it wasn't hard to find those reasons."

Molly looked at Ty. She'd hated him for so long, it was hard to see him any other way. But looking at him now, Molly saw an ordinary man in a wet suit who didn't believe in himself and took it out on other people. There was nothing to be angry at. Ty Spencer was his own worst enemy. If he wants to apologize, Molly thought, I'll accept it. Maybe this is the first step on the road to a whole new Ty Spencer.

If he could change the way he looked at

things, then anything could change. "Okay, Spencer," she said. "I accept your apology. And I apologize for calling you a big fat liar." She smiled hesitantly and extended her hand. Ty shook it.

A tow truck that Irene had called on her cell phone pulled up to take Ty's car. He began to walk over to it. "Hey, Spencer?" Molly called. He turned around. "Who was it who made you see what you were doing?" she asked.

Ty gave her a look of surprise. "Your daughter told me," he said. "It was this afternoon, right after you left. She's a pretty amazing kid." Ty turned and walked away.

Molly watched him go in complete amazement. So Fi was responsible! How had Fi managed to change someone who had been so angry for so long, so quickly? She guessed it was just part of who her daughter was. Molly turned and saw Fi standing in the road with a big blanket wrapped around her. She looked so small out on the highway, but Molly thought she towered over everyone in spirit.

Fi watched Ty talking to the tow truck driver. His car looked like an ancient heap of junk. She wondered how he would get home. Ty glanced in her direction and saw her. Was he still mad at her,

Fi wondered? Why had he been out on the highway that night? Ty walked slowly over to her. "I didn't know Molly Phillips had a daughter," he said.

Fi shrugged. "That's me. I guess you're pretty mad about your car, huh?"

Ty glanced over at the tow truck. "It's no big deal," he said. "People are more important than cars. I'm just glad everyone's all right." Ty smiled at Fi. It was a little strange. She'd never seen him smile. It didn't look like something he did often, but Fi smiled back. "Good luck on your tour," Ty said. "I'll be rooting for you."

Fi watched as the tow truck driver hooked up Ty's car. This was so weird.

Later, Ned, Irene, Clu, and Jack watched as the tow truck pulled Ty's car away. Fi sat on the bottom step of the bus in the open doorway. It had started to rain again, and she had wrapped herself in her dad's old suede jacket. She was so confused about everything that had happened. The prediction on the Web site had come true, but she still didn't know why it had been sent to her, or who had sent it.

Molly walked over to Fi carrying an umbrella. She kneeled down in front of Fi and looked seriously into her eyes. "You really saved the day," Molly said.

Fi shrugged. "I don't know how I did it."

"I was talking to Ty Spencer," said Molly. "Do you know why he was out here tonight?"

Fi shook her head.

"He was trying to catch up with us. So he could apologize for everything."

Fi stared at her mother. "He apologized?" she said. "But what happened to make him change his mind?"

Molly gave her daughter a knowing smile. "It seems someone made Ty Spencer see that music is about making people happy. He thought he'd start making people happy, too."

Fi was amazed. Did Ty Spencer actually decide to apologize because of what she said to him?

"He was coming to our concert in Deer Falls," Molly said. "But his car stalled on the road. He didn't have any flares . . ."

Fi nodded, still trying to figure out what this all meant. Molly reached out and cupped her chin, turning Fi's face to meet her own. "You saved his life, baby," she said seriously. "You know what that means?"

Fi wasn't sure she did. It seemed impossible that she had had such an effect on him when she had only met him once. Would Ty have died if it hadn't been for her? Maybe that was the way Fate worked. It put the right people together at the right time.

"Mommy?" Fi said, looking up into her mother's eyes.

"Yes, baby?"

"Does everything happen for a reason?"

Molly looked away. Fi's question was one she'd asked herself many times since Rick had died. She had never been able to find an answer for herself. "I don't know," Molly said quietly. "But I do know that you are an amazing person. And every time you go out in the world, you're going to make a difference. You have already. More than you know."

Molly gave Fi a kiss. "Let's get some sleep," she said, hurrying Fi up the stairs.

"Okay," said Fi. She watched her mom walk back to Ned and Irene, who were checking the tires of the bus.

Looking at them, it seemed to Fi that things had to happen for a reason. It seemed that everything had been arranged from the start so that they would all end up together on this road. Was someone looking out for them, protecting them from harm that night?

Had this been what the Webmaster had wanted all along?

Chapter Sixteen

Fi climbed into the bus and opened the closet in the common room. She carefully hung her dad's jacket on a hanger inside. Behind her, Molly came onto the bus, followed by Ned and Irene.

"I can't believe Ty Spencer apologized," Ned said. "Somebody pinch me."

"We've got Fi to thank for it," said Molly. "She was the one who managed to get through to the human being in him."

Irene and Ned stared at Fi in astonishment. "Fi?" said Irene. "How did you do it?"

Fi thought about it. She really wasn't sure. All she'd done is tell him how happy her mother's music made people and suggested that he could make people happy too if he tried. "I just told him the truth," she said finally. "I guess he listened."

"You make it sound easy," said Ned. "People have tried to get that guy to listen for years."

"He'd never met Fi before," Molly said proudly, putting her arm around Fi's shoulder. "She's going to change the world."

Ned smiled and stretched, ready to get on the road again. "Where are the boys?" he asked.

Irene glanced out the window. "I think they're getting footage of the skidmarks or something."

Fi rolled her eyes. "I'll get 'em," she said, grabbing an umbrella.

The highway was empty when Fi got outside. There was no trace of the near disaster left on the road. "Clu!" she called. "Clu! Jack! Come on, we're ready to go."

Fi heard a rustling in the bushes at the side of the road and jumped. "Hello?" she said. "Is anyone out there?" Fi took a step toward the side of the road.

From the bushes she heard three voices in quick succession. The first was Clu's. "There he is!"

The second was Jack's. "Get him!"

The third belonged to an angry raccoon that hissed and came barreling out into the road followed by the two filmmakers. Clu was humming the theme to *Wild Kingdom* as he sprinted after the animal. Jack filmed it all with the video camera.

"Fi! Head him off!" yelled Clu.

Fi glared at them. "Leave the raccoon alone!" she said.

Jack took the camera away from his face and looked at Fi as if she'd hurt his feelings.

"Don't worry," said Clu. "No animals were harmed during the making of this documentary."

"We're doing this for you, you know, Fi," he said. "We thought we were tracking Bigfoot . . . for your Web site!"

"I've got enough visitors to my Web site, thank you very much," said Fi. She couldn't believe that she had just practically proven that someone could predict the future and Clu and Jack were out here chasing raccoons around the highway. "Come on," she said. "Ned's getting ready to leave."

With one last glance at the bushes, Clu and Jack followed Fi back to the bus. Within an hour they were headed toward Deer Falls again. Fi, Clu, and Jack sat around the table drinking hot chocolate because it was too weird to sleep. Clu was showing Fi all the footage he and Jack had shot earlier in the evening.

When Fi saw the video Jack had shot out the bus window she started getting goose bumps. There was the sign, just as in the video she saw on her computer, saying Rockville was thirty miles away. Right after that Fi saw herself standing outside of her room asking Jack what was going on. Her face looked pale and strange, as if she was scared to death. "What was the matter with you?"

asked Jack, looking at the monitor over her shoulder. "You looked like you saw a ghost."

"I don't know what I saw," said Fi. "I was sleeping and my computer turned on by itself. Somebody sent me a video file that started playing on my computer. It was the same video I saw in the *Dillon Dispatch* office. It showed a bus passing by the Rockville sign and then crashing into a car—Ty Spencer's car. I knew we were going to crash, so I ran up to the driver's seat to warn Ned."

"Cool," said Clu. "Premonition of Demolition!"

"Premonition?" said Jack, obviously still unconvinced. "Fi, you were sleeping. You had a dream. Computers can't turn themselves on. You've been freaked out about this bus crash idea all day and you dreamed about it. I'm sure glad you did, because you did save all our lives, but it was still a coincidence."

"Don't close your eyes to the truth," said Fi.

Jack frowned. "What does that mean?"

"That was my horoscope today. I checked it before I went to sleep."

"What does that prove?" said Jack.

Clu bounced up and went to Fi's room to grab *The Dillon Dispatch*. This horoscope thing was getting interesting.

"Listen, Fi," said Jack. "The only reason horoscopes seem to tell the future is because you only remember the ones that come true. Unless my horoscope says I'd better finish my American Lit paper by tomorrow, I'm not buying it."

"Finish overdue work now or face the consequences," said Clu.

Jack turned around. "Excuse me?"

Clu started laughing. "Dude, that was your horoscope," he said, pointing to the paper he had gotten out of Fi's room. "You're totally busted!"

Fi looked from Clu to Jack and then broke into a grin. Jack frowned, embarrassed, and grabbed the paper from Clu. Sure enough, that was his horoscope. He still didn't believe in astrology, but he had to give this one to Fi. "Okay, that's a pretty lucky coincidence," said Jack. "But I still don't think the Unknown Webmaster knows everything that's going to happen before it happens. Remember, the Webmaster said that our bus was going to crash, and it didn't."

"Yeah, because of Fi's excellent driving," said Clu. "Way to cut a sharp right!"

Fi was beginning to think the guys would never see the point here. "I wouldn't have known what to do if the Webmaster hadn't sent me that video of the future," she said. "The only thing I don't understand is why he sent it to me."

Clu and Jack looked at each other and shrugged. They didn't have any answer.

Later Fi got ready for bed and opened up the Current Investigations file on her Web site. She looked over all of the strange messages she'd gotten from Unknown and everything she'd seen on the Web site and recorded in the file. Everything seemed to lead up to Fi saving Ty Spencer. *But how important is one life?* Fi typed on her keyboard. *Did all this happen just so I could save that guy who wrote mean stuff about Mom?*

Who would want to do that? Did the Webmaster know who Fi was? *Who sent those messages?* Fi wrote. She chewed on her lip and looked up at the picture of her father, holding Fi in his arms when she was a baby. *Could it have been Dad?* Fi wrote. *Or is Jack right? Is he gone forever?*

Fi looked back at the computer screen. *I guess some things do happen for a reason,* she wrote. *But can we ever know what the reason is? Did Ty Spencer have someone looking out for him? Or did I? Does everyone?* Fi shook her head, logged off, and got into bed.

She looked across the room at the picture of

her father. As she looked at the picture, she heard her computer click on-line again all by itself. "You have mail," the computer voice announced.

"This is so weird," Fi muttered.

Fi got out of bed, went to her computer, and clicked on the Communications icon of her Web site. "Unknown!" she said, looking at the sender line. "I didn't think I'd hear from you again." The subject line was blank as usual. "Who are you?" Fi said out loud, getting angry now. "Who are you?"

In the text portion of the message, Fi read: "On September 16 you wrote: *Can we change it?*"

Fi frowned. That was the message she had sent Unknown in the *Dillon Dispatch* office right after he had first shown her the video of the bus crashing. She waited for an answer.

"You can change anything," came the reply. Fi read the message and slowly began to smile. She clicked on the reply button.

"Who are you?" she whispered. Instead of a reply window, a box popped up with the message: Error—Sender does not exist.

Fi reached out and touched the screen. She knew all she needed to know. She knew that there was someone out there who would always be there for her and always believe in her.

Maybe she really could change anything.

Epilogue

The Molly Phillips tour bus reached the outskirts of Deer Falls just as the sun rose. Fi slept peacefully in her bed. No dreams disturbed her. She continued to sleep as her computer opened silently on her desk. "Logging on."

The familiar eyeball appeared on the screen at Fi's Web page.

The cursor moved quickly across the screen, searching for the icon for Current Investigations. The cursor clicked on the folder name and the keys moved silently, as if invisible fingers were touching them. When they were finished, the folder had been renamed: Case Closed.